Broken Biscuits : The Wood Fairy

Ian Colquhoun

Copyright © 2025 by Ian Colquhoun

All rights reserved.

No part of this publication may be reproduced, distributed, or transmitted in any form or by any means, including photocopying, recording, or other electronic or mechanical methods, without the prior written permission of the publisher, except as permitted by U.S. copyright law. For permission requests, contact Ian Colquhoun.

The story, all names, characters, and incidents portrayed in this production are fictitious. No identification with actual persons (living or deceased), places, buildings, and products is intended or should be inferred.

Edited by: Lindsay Drummond
Formatted by: Sienna Arts

1st edition 2025

Contents

Dedication	V
About this Book	VI
Acknowledgements	VIII
Prologue: The Love I Lost	IX
1. Bits 'N' Pieces	1
2. Mindcircus	4
3. Seven Cities	9
4. The Awakening	16
5. House Arrest	23
6. Cry	28
7. Lizard	34
8. Castles in the Sky	37
9. Southern Sun	46
10. Take Me Away	51
11. Feeling This Way	57
12. Pearl River	60

13.	We Are Alive	65
14.	We Are Alive, Part Two : Disco's Revenge	72
15.	Bla Bla Bla	86
16.	Nothing But You	89
17.	For An Angel	95
18.	Synths and Strings	98
19.	Proximus	106
20.	Not Over Yet	114
21.	Fly Away	116
22.	Take The Long Way Home	119
23.	Café Del Mar	124
24.	Strange World	133
25.	Manumission	139
26.	CODA	150
ABOUT THE AUTHOR		152

To my God-daughter, Kerry

About this Book

The ideas for this story and for this wider new series appeared in my head a few years ago – I could see and hear one of the characters that you're about to meet, in my head.

My AuDHD diagnosis from 2023, though a shock in some ways, has allowed me to unleash my imagination, whereas in the past as I wrote I was unwittingly masking, afraid of my imagination and thus trying to be neurotypical. I hope that the reader appreciates the change of direction .

This new series of books, Broken Biscuits, is set in the hinterland of Scotland in between the two main cities – the many towns and villages along the M8 and in Lanarkshire, West Lothian and the general central belt. Most locations are real. No characters are based on real people.

Broken Biscuits are people from working class housing estates, or *schemes*, as we call them in Scotland. We grew up in the post 1980s neoliberal wasteland, a transitional post-industrial era in which began the drugs plague, a plague which still infects our country today.

For the most part, there are three types of person born in the schemes. Some don't make it, their lives cut short by violent crime, poverty or by drugs – either directly or indirectly.

Some get away, be it via study, work or marriage – they escape. Most of us, however, stay in or near the places that we grew up in, surviving and thriving, making lives for ourselves in spite of the two-pronged assault that we face, from drugs and organised crime on the one hand, and from indifferent politicians and under-funded public services on the other.

We are the Broken Biscuits that neoliberalism left behind.

It's not a derogatory term, at all. After all, broken biscuits, though often rough around the edges, are usually the best in the world – and we know how to have a laugh.

Acknowledgements

I should like to acknowledge and thank the following people for their help, inspiration or support in this new thing.

My superb editor, Lindsay Drummond. My family and close friends for their encouragement. Those publishers who declined the series yet still took time to give me constructive, helpful feedback.

Tony, Maggie, Jenny, Davie, Barton, Paul Larkin, Steve Richards, Bobby Sinnet, Paul, Ellie, Josie, Amanda, Big Gary, Angela the raver, Shug, RTN Healthcare, Heather, Gemma, Kerry and Brian, Ronnie, Sir Tom Farmer, Gemma, John, Sam Agnew, Sara Ferris, Ollie Hancock, Stuart Penn, Dr Chris Brown, and my beloved cat, Jack.

Prologue: The Love I Lost

Manchester in 1989, the summer of love, and what a summer it promised to be. I'm from Glasgow but I was staying doon there doing a postgraduate degree at UMIST. Classes were over for the summer, and I was out on the town with friends: Leanne, Charlotte, and Blair. Blair is Scottish, too, like me, and a student and he's pretty sound, for a white lad. We share a flat. Leanne is from Wigan and is Blair's other half, she's sound. Charlotte is something else, beautiful, funny, smart – and posh; her folks live in nearby Hale. We've snogged a few times but that's as far as it's went so far – to be honest, we're all about the weekends – we're the four musketeers.

So, yeah, we're in Manchester, or *Madchester*, as folks are calling it now, and on this particular Friday night, we're in the Hacienda – that's right, the fuckin' Hacienda! Top one, as they say down here. See, we all love house music, and we love to party, so this place is fuckin' paradise. We're at *Nude*, Britain's first regular house-music club night. Every Friday over a thousand like-minded souls descend on this mecca of hedonism and loved up madness. Fuck other nightclubs, with their lager louts, handbag dancing, punch-ups, and shite music – fuck them, that's not a good time, that's how the old generation did weekends – our generation needs something else and, boy, have we got it. The four of us started coming to the Hacienda about a year ago and it's changed our lives. The place, the people, the drugs; it's all opened our minds so much. The only downside is that the lifestyle of 36-hour weekends has messed with our studies a bit, but really, who cares, who actually becomes a student in order to get qualifications? Mugs!

So, aye, we're cutting some shapes on the dancefloor in the Hacienda on this Friday night, early in May 1989, havin' it large. I'm wearing my baggy flared jeans, a white *Moschino* tee-shirt and a pair of brown *Pony* trainers that look like dress shoes. Mike Pickering is on the decks, he is the prophet, we are his apostles, man. The night is going well; we've, the four of us, had half a dove each and the weekend has landed, big time. The DJ plays '*Dirty Cash*' by Stevie V and the place is erupting, man. Then everyone loses it even more when he spins a cool white-label mix of 'People Hold On' by Coldcut – with me pretty certain that I'd been talking to the vocalist from that track in here the other week, a lass called Lisa Stansfield – she's dead nice – I totally failed to get off with her.

The dancefloor is just one loving, single organism for the whole night. My three pals and I meet loads of amazing people, old faces and new. The only downside to the night comes when I walk straight into one of the bollards beside the dancefloor, crushing my balls. I double over in agony, but my friends are laughing so hard that I soon forget my pain. This is what it's all about, the summer of love – the dancefloor, party drugs, love, and good people. It's been an epic night, once again. And yet, even this wonderful place has to close for the night, so we find ourselves back at this mental party in someone's big old house in Salford, where we can at last smoke some weed and chill. The house belongs to two rich Manc guys that Blair knows, they're sound. There's about 15 people in the house and a guy is spinning the decks, playing my favourite house track, 'That's the way love is' by Ten City, I pure dig that bassline, man.

That's the way love is
That's the way love is
That's the way love is

As the quality tunes and the chat flow, two of the birds at the party – I keep forgetting their names but they're sound – bring round these tiny wee white cups for everybody. At first, Ah'm like yes, more drink, but it's not, it's mushy tea – that's liquid LSD brewed from psychedelic magic mushrooms, in case you're wonderin'. Everybody batters into their share of the 'tea' – though everybody is already wasted on various uppers, weed and alcohol, anyway. About an hour after this, everything becomes, well, a bit of a blur. We're now well into Saturday morning and everybody is utterly melted. The guys whose house it is take a phone call and, after briefing their party guests, herd all 15 of us into two cars and a camper van. We head north to go to an all-day party in Glasgow. Me, Blair, Charlotte, and Leanne don't have a motor, so someone hands us the keys to a flashy Sierra Cosworth RS! The boy said he was too wasted to drive, like. And we weren't?

I agreed to drive the thing after some persuasion from Blair 'n' that. Blair rode shotgun and Leanne and Charlotte sat in the back. Nobody had any maps but Manchester to Glasgow isn't hard, and the rich lads from the house knew where to go when we got up there. I could drive, but I didn't even have a license. We made it up to Glasgow in convoy just fine, though I did have a quality argument with Blair en route. He digs out the bag of pink champagne and everybody has a dab except me. I tried explaining that I was trippin' ma nuts off and really didn't need any more drugs, but Blair reckoned the speed would make me more alert. In the end, I had a tiny dab, just to shut him up, but for the rest of the drive I was imagining what would happen if the polis pulled us over, and realised the driver was a young black man, off his tits, nae license or insurance – what was I meant to say to them?

'Aye officer, listen, it's all cool cos I've just took some good Lou Reed to straighten me up a bit,' – they'd have kicked my cunt in, then thrown away the fuckin' key.

The party in Glasgow was good, a big gathering in somebody's garden in Milngavie. Us Scots know how to party, but a few hours into that Glasgow party, these other hippies invited us through to Edinburgh, to go to an all-night secret outdoor rave in a place called Blackford Quarry. It seemed like everybody at this Glesga party was heading through there, so we agreed to go, too.

Not everybody at this Glasgow party was a sound cunt, though. There were three dudes and a lassie in who just didn't fit in. They weren't hippies or ravers, they looked and acted more like drug dealers and young wannabe gangsters, sitting together in their wee clique. I think it was them who had brought through most of the Es that were being consumed at this party. They were from one of those dreadful medium-sized towns that lie on the main road between Glasgow and Edinburgh, judging by their accents. There are always arseholes at big parties, though, and on another day, this wouldn't have mattered. On any other fuckin' day.

Blair's girlfriend, Leanne, went into the big house to use the toilet. On the way back from the bog she bumped into the kind of leader of the early 20s out-of-town gangster clique, on the stairs. Initially, this guy tried to chat Leanne up, then he offered her more drugs, but Leanne had just smiled and brushed past him. He'd grabbed her by the arm and tried to pull her in for a kiss as she passed, but Leanne had pulled away in time, told him she had a boyfriend, and he'd replied with degrading insults.

BROKEN BISCUITS : THE WOOD FAIRY

Leanne had come back out to the garden and told Blair, Charlotte, and me. Blair asked two of the hippies who this guy was, and it was confirmed that this guy was an up-and-coming wannabe gangster from the central belt, named Gavin. As Gavin and his lot were also supposed to be heading through to the Blackford Quarry rave in Edinburgh later, we all decided just to forget the incident, for harmony's sake – everybody was wasted, after all.

But, about an hour later, as everybody danced, drank, and partied in the May sunshine to *'Got to have your love'* by Mantronix, this Gavin started his pish again.

Boy, I got to have your love
(Gotta find a way to get into your heart)
You know, you know, you know I need your love
(Gotta find a way to get into your heart)

This Gavin started dancing closer to us and kept banging into Leanne's man, Blair. Blair was no fighter and was a nice guy, but after the fifth time of being barged into, he told this Gavin

'Watch where yer fuckin' goin', mate.'

'I'm no' yer mate,' replied Gavin, and he threw a punch at Blair, catching him just under the eye, but not knocking him over. This Gavin had clearly planned the whole incident, revenge for Leanne rebuffing him on the stairs. I instinctively stepped over to protect my mate and pushed this Gavin in the chest with both hands, telling him to back the fuck off. By now, the whole party were staring at the standoff. Gavin was more drunk than wasted, he took a swing at me, calling me a 'fucking nigger bastard' as he swung, but I sidestepped it and managed to kick him in the balls. He doubled over, winded, as his troglodyte mates came over to back him up.

Blair was now standing beside me, and we faced these dickheads down. Gavin kept mouthing off.

'You'll regret this, both of ye, and they two slags you're with, you're aw fuckin' deed.'

'Come ahead, then, just you and me,' I said to him.

He was actually rather bigger than me and I was totally unsure if I'd be able to take him, then I noticed him reach for his back pocket. As he did, one of his mates grabbed his arm and said to him, 'No' here, Gav, later, mate, later, think of the business.'

Gavin's hand moved away from his back pocket, but he continued staring at me. Then, the couple whose garden we were partying in finally decided to step in. They spoke quietly to that Gavin and his friends, who promptly left. Then the couple, themselves pure hippies in their 40s, came over to us, and the guy said, 'Sorry about that, we know that wasn't your fault, we needed Es today for this wee gathering and that Neanderthal was a necessary evil, in that respect. Don't worry, he won't be at the Blackford Quarry thing now, either. We know his boss. Well done, by the way, you've just humiliated the right-hand-man of one of Scotland's biggest drug dealers!'

Although we weren't at fault, we apologised to them, but they knew whose fault the altercation had been. I asked them if I should take the threat seriously, to which the hippie guy's wife replied

'Yes, yes, you should. We'll have a word with his boss, but that guy is a fucking psycho. We're lucky he didn't bring out that big folding knife he carries.'

I knew he'd had a fucking knife! Cowardly scumbag.

This incident didn't ruin the party, in fact, everybody was relieved that Gavin and his minions were gone. We all dropped more acid before we started getting ready to drive through to this outdoor rave in Edinburgh.

BROKEN BISCUITS : THE WOOD FAIRY

We were all beyond wasted. Soon, me, Blair, Charlotte, and Leanne were back in the Sierra Cosworth, as part of another convoy, this time the destination was Edinburgh. The drugs we were carrying through to the rave were in the boot of the car and we were listening to *The twelve commandments of dance* album by the London Boys as we drove along the M8. The awesome track, 'Requiem', was playing. We'd seen them play the Hacienda a few weeks earlier. They were a bit G.A.Y. Disco for my taste, but the tracks were still good.

You're the love of my life, my life, my life
And I won't let you go now
This is a requiem for love
Our love, our love is a miracle now, oh
Like a thief in the night, the night, the night
I was begging for love
This is a requiem for –
Life has set me free, taking a chance on you and me
This is the story now
The story of our love

As our convoy traversed the M8, I looked in the rearview mirror just before we reached Coatbridge and saw two police panda cars behind us. Talk about getting fuckin' paranoid!

By the time we reached the Whitburn junction they were still there, and we were all starting to panic – utter paranoia. I decided to come off the M8 at Bathgate, as splitting our convoy would make us harder to follow, but one cop car followed us. Their shitey panda car could follow but not catch us, and we drove up into some hills behind Bathgate to try and get away from them. We stopped at some iron-age site, still out of our faces, and tried our hand at ancient Celtic Druid dance rituals, on that hot, sunny Saturday in May 1989. It was while up that hill, with a near 360-degree view of central Scotland all around us, that I had a moment of the utmost clarity; that Gavin and his mates had sent the polis. The snide had grassed us up! Revenge for our slight on him and his crew, the heinous crime of not tolerating any of his pish. We were aw ragin'. Fuckin' incandescent. What really ripped ma knittin' about it was that the grass was himself a drug dealer, or a gangster, or whatever – they're no' supposed to dae that.

We bumped into the polis again on the way down the hill and had to ditch the car and split up to avoid capture. I ended up running into some sort of country park picnic area, still severely para and utterly melted. Some tidy hillwalker bird I bumped into there, took advantage of my wasted state, prick-teased me and offered to help me escape from the cops, and then, well...

Oh, by the way, my name's Sandy ... and now I'm fuckin' ragin'...

Chapter One

Bits 'N' Pieces

Central Scotland in 1999 could be pretty dull, tedious even, especially if you were young. We had the wild weekends, though. Labour had recently been elected and, for the first few years of Tony Blair's Britain, it seemed that most people had a little bit more money to spend, more people had decent jobs and folk were, well, less angry in general. It was most definitely, for club 18–30, party time.

In just five short years, the rave/house scene had gone from being a feared pariah, organised by shady characters and held in dangerous shithole venues, with its every aspect vilified by the media, to being the lifeblood of new, cool Britannia, influencing fashion, popular culture and social attitudes alike. Of course, the establishment exerted its own tax on young people, for normalising their culture and making it both accessible and acceptable. If you want to go partying in the new superclubs, be they in Glasgow, Bathgate, or Perth, you'll no' be getting into the fucking place unless you're wearing designer gear, or at the very least, coloured jeans and a casual shirt, without trainers. The rules are different for women. As far as nightclub owners and bouncers see it, less is more. Just wear a short skirt and don't look younger than Shirley fuckin' Temple and you're in.

If you want to enjoy the establishment's new sanitised version of the rave, you'll be drinking alcohol, too. After all, nightclub promoters cannae make any money just off your £10 entry fee, eh? The fact that drinking beer, popping Es, dancing, sweating, and wearing designer gear all at the same time is a complete contradiction of the ego-free early-90s rave culture is conveniently ignored by everybody, because that suits everybody. That's fashion. That's a way of life. Nobody does religion anymore. As the great Maxi Jazz once said, 'This *is my church. This is where I heal my hurt. For tonight, God is a DJ.*'

Two avid members of the Church of Sweatbox Laserbeam are Colin and Stevie, both aged 20, both average height. Stevie has short, blonde, curly hair, Colin has dark hair but keeps it shaved right down to the wood. Both are skinny as fuck – like most clubbers at their peak are. Stevie works on the production line at a Mitsubishi plant, while Colin earns his own pittance in a large food distribution centre, in the same industrial estate. Both their jobs are poorly paid, like almost all jobs for so-called 'unskilled' workers are. The age-old problem of the cunt in charge in the office doing sweet fuck-all all day, every day, while those under his charge work their arse off for a pittance won't be resolved by the looming end of the 20th century, either. However, by the time they pay their digs on a Friday, these two likely lads have enough money left to go absolutely fuckin' radio rental all weekend, most weekends, with their usual crew of friends and associates. Weekdays are for working, recovery from the previous weekend, and for shaggin' women. Weekends are for manumission.

It's a wonderful word that, eh? Manumission. Originally it refers to the 'freedom papers' given to black former-slaves in pre-1865 America. Manumisson = freedom from slavery. No more being ordered around and owned and terrorised by a wanker of a boss, free to be yourself and to do whatever the fuck you want. Whoever named that big nightclub in Ibiza Manumission picked the most apt name for their establishment, that's for sure. In fact, by 1999, all clubbing is a form of manumission – freedom from neoliberal exploitation, freedom from dull routine, freedom from that tosser supervisor at your work whose hideous breath smells like he has eaten a big plate of fresh shite for his breakfast. Freedom, at least, for a couple of days. Those 60 hours or so when you're free from the humdrums must be made the most of. Life is short, seize the day, all that cliché shite.

In housing schemes in modern Britain, there are three types of kids, you see. Three trajectories for young life in our neoliberal world. Some die young via drugs, deprivation, or violent crime. Some lucky ones get away from the ghetto and forge decent lives. The ones who remain, who survive the scheme and make their lives still in or near the ghetto, we are the broken biscuits – the unwanted, the inconvenient truth – neoliberalism's children of the damned. Billionaires thrive while we pay for it all. But, despite the hardships that we face through drugs gangs, shite wages, shithole expensive housing, useless policing and ever-decreasing public services, we make the most of things. That's all we can do – we make the most of what we have. Colin and Stevie are two of these broken biscuits.

Chapter Two

Mindcircus

This particular April weekend, Colin and Stevie have been out partying but neither of them feels like they are making the most of anything. At all.

Friday night had seen them, and a large group of friends, head to Bathgate in a fleet of cars – including Colin's snazzy white Peugeot 205. Stevie didn't drive. The group of 12 friends had arrived at the popular *'Room at the Top'* venue with the guys looking like male models, in razor-ironed shirts and Firetrap jeans, with Rockport shoes, and the lassies looking like beautiful pop stars in their clubbing gear. Of course, by the time they all left the place at near 4am, the drink, the drugs, the endless sweating and a combination of dancefloor smoke effects and the huge cloud of fag smoke which enveloped that dancefloor had them looking less like supermodels and more like a fuckin' zombie apocalypse. Smudged makeup, crumpled shirts, drink stains, fag burns, even stains from leaning against the club's manky walls – but of course, nothing made them look rougher than the expressions on their happy, buzzing yet utterly melted faces. The music had been good all night – no big names on a Friday there, but local heroes Martin Malone and Paul Mendez had had the place bouncin', as they always did. Musical highlight of the evening had been

700 pairs of hands in the air in room one to an epic mix of 'Happiness Happening' by Lost Witness.

Everything will be perfect
Everything will be perfect
Everything will be perfect
Tonight and forever

After the club, most of them made for a house party in Longridge – a desolate ex-mining town on the border of West Lothian and South Lanarkshire. The party was enjoyed by all, more pills were consumed, a lot of soap bar was smoked, hours more of great tunes kept the party pilot light on well into Saturday morning. Not many at the party kept drinking, most were sipping water or drinking cups of tea made by the party host's zany but likable wife. When that party had run its course, Colin and Stevie left, offering a lift home to two of the lassies from their housing scheme they both really liked, Kirsty and Clare, who were slightly older than them. The four of them had been hanging out together frequently of late, as mates. They had all ended up going back to Kirsty's flat, where joints were rolled and a more relaxed, intimate party carried on, with MTV Dance playing on the huge 26-inch TV. Clare had to work the next evening, she was a barmaid, and by 10am she wanted to go home. Clare was cute, with short dark hair, brown eyes, and a dark complexion. She had an infectious smile, even when melted. Colin, who was by now feeling rough and tired, offered to drive her home and she accepted.

A lot of people get very horny when the comedown stage kicks in, and these four clubbers were no different. Colin gave Stevie a wink as he picked up the car keys and headed off with Clare, leaving Stevie alone in the flat with Kirsty, a voluptuous, hedonistic blonde who had once been a dancer for rave band, N-Joi, back in the day.

'I'm in love with you. Want you to love me, too'

Alas, Cupid's arrow was to fall short for these four clubbers, that Saturday morning in 1999.

Colin managed to drive Clare home safely, overcoming his intense paranoia that every other car on the road was an unmarked polis car, specifically looking for him. As they got to Clare's front door, Clare started to be sick; violently, and loudly. She vomited so hard that the light brown, repulsive stream of sick hit the pavement and bounced back up and all over Colin's jeans and Rockports. Colin, worried about her wellbeing but also slightly irked inside that this poorly timed spewing sesh had ruined his chance to seduce this seriously sexy woman, did the only thing that he could do. He took Clare's keys and helped her into her house, laying her on the sofa and fetching a basin from the sink for her to spew into. And spew she did. Again, and again. He got her a glass of water and sat in the armchair opposite her, where he remained for a few hours, until he was sure that she was okay.

When she had recomposed herself a bit, Colin took her through to her bed then returned to the lounge. He emptied the spew basin and lay down on the sofa. He'd left Clare's bedroom door open, in case she needed help. She had mumbled to him, 'wake me at 6pm for work', and to his surprise, at 6pm on the dot, Clare was up, showered, drinking tea and eating toast before heading away to do her shift. Colin had spent the last few hours watching cartoons on the telly, drifting in and out of a kind of half-sleep. He declined Clare's invitation for him to come and keep her company in the bar that evening, the last place Colin could handle was a pub right now.

After dropping Clare at her work, Colin headed home, to get out of his vomit-encrusted clobber, have a shower, and maybe even avert a nervous breakdown.

Stevie had fared no better. Kirsty had suggested that they both take the edge off their looming hangover-comedowns by having hash yoghurts. This involved getting a tablespoonful of vegetable oil and heating it on the hob, then adding some chopped up hash to the oil, melting them together in the spoon, then tipping the black, bubbling mixture into a Petit Filous yoghurt and eating it. Within around 30 minutes of them wolfing down this merry sludge, both were on the sofa, giggling, hugging, and kissing. And then … nothing.

Stevie woke on the sofa a few hours later, groggy, dizzy, hungry, and puzzled. The hash yoghurt had completely overridden everything else that they had consumed over the last 12 hours or so, and they had both fallen asleep at the exact same time. Kirsty, snoring away, was hogging most of the sofa, but that was okay. The MTV Dance channel on the TV was still on, and Stevie knew that it was the dreadful drum 'n' bass hour on it that had woken him up – Scotland didn't really 'do' jungle. That *wasn't* okay. Stevie got up to grab the SKY remote and ended up waking Kirsty, who seemed pleased to see him, if a little confused.

Smiling, Kirsty spoke.

'Listen, Stevie, I'm workin' the morra, it's been a blast, man, but I need to take some time oot to pick up the pieces. I need my bed, I need sleep, like, to actually sleep, ken.'

'Nae bother, Kirsty,' replied Stevie. He knew. Neither of them was in any fit state to do anything else. Kirsty looked like she'd been awake for days. He was sweating and looked ten times worse than she did. She still looked beautiful, though.

'Fire up during the week one night when we're both in better shape, but, and we'll carry on where we left off,' continued Kirsty, matter-of-factly.

'Aye, sounds good tae me, Ah'm burst anyway, Kirsty, I best be on ma way. I'll phone ye during the week.'

'Ye better,' snapped Kirsty.

'Ah will,' said Stevie, with a cheeky smile. The two shared a kiss and one last hug, before Stevie was on his way.

What Stevie really needed was a bath, a change of clothes and some food. Kirsty's flat wasn't far from where he lived and, as it was a sunny day, he walked home, rather than getting a taxi.

He soon regretted that decision. As he trudged home through the housing schemes in his crumpled, stained clothes from last night smelling of BO, fags, drink, and weed, his short, blonde hair matted in sweat and pure hummin', and his eyes as wide as flying saucers, he felt like a fucking tramp, as he passed sprightly dog-walkers, mums with small children and OAPs out for a stroll to SPAR. He was sure they were all talking about him as he passed. Nobody made eye contact, everybody walked on the other side of the footpath to avoid him. That, my friends, is called the walk of shame.

Chapter Three

Seven Cities

Stevie got home, his parents were out, thankfully, so, he ran a bath, smoking a joint out of his open bedroom window while he waited for the bath to fill, then he sat for a long time in the water. A bath feels horrible when you've been melted, really horrible, for some reason, but the hot water also relaxed his muscles, and he was able to sleep for a few hours after it.

At around 7pm, the doorbell rang, and Stevie stumbled downstairs to answer it. It was Colin, and he looked dressed to go out, again...

Despite the fragile state that they were both in, Colin and Stevie quickly agreed that it was in their best interests to go out again that night. There was a big night on at The Arches in Glasgow, a Beat 106 FM special with DJs Trevor Reilly and Simon Foy. Colin was okay to drive, having had a couple of hours sleep. They each drank a bottle of Budweiser in the kitchen at Stevie's house, then jumped into the flashy white Peugeot 205 and hit the M8, Glasgow bound, with a pirated CD blaring all the way.

Colin actually hated Simon Foy. He'd never met the guy but had once been at an afterparty in South Queensferry where an eccied party host had went on and on about being pals with that particular DJ, repeating the story over and over again, as pillheads often do. Colin had gotten so sick of the cunt slavering about Simon Foy for hours that he had considered lamping the boy – something you just don't do to folk in the dance/rave scene. In the end, he had left the party just to get away from the Simon Foy slaver, and in the process had ruined his chances of pulling wee Davina, a clubhead lassie from Edinburgh whom, on more than one occasion, he had totally failed to get off with at various house parties.

The Arches was mobbed. The queue was huge. End of the month – payday.

The wonderful old venue – a disused railway yard converted into a multi-room dance-music venue – reverberated to pounding bass and was, like *Room at the Top* the night before, full of snappily dressed fellas dripping with designer clothing, and scantily dressed, beautiful, bodacious young women, all out for a hedonistic good time, and all out of their faces. The place was rockin'. Nowhere else in Britain does euphoric trance and techno nights quite like Scotland does, and that's a pure fact.

Colin and Stevie soon managed to buy six eccies off some lanky fucker in the corner, who was about as inconspicuous as a polar bear trying to gain entry to a 'penguins only' disco. This meant that the boy was one of the venue's approved dealers and neither he nor his customers would face any bother from the bouncers. It was a different story for any outsiders caught trying to flog pills in someone's club, though – they'd get huckled, their pills taken, and then either leathered by the bouncers or have the police phoned. It sometimes suited venues more to get the cops to these outsiders, it looked good for their facade of being anti-drugs.

Lanky pill seller had quoted Colin and Stevie a tenner a pill. In Scotland in 1999, this was almost always met with an *'aw fuck off'* from whoever was trying to buy the pills. They soon haggled the guy down to the socially acceptable fiver per pill. The pills were flogged to them as 'Rainbow Brites' as they were pink and white speckled and featured a stamped image of a matchstick wee girl on them. They washed a pill each down with their bottles of water – neither could face anymore bevvy that weekend. Within half an hour, neither was really feeling anything. As the party continued all around them and hundreds of melted people strutted their stuff, all they did was sweat.

'Another one?' shouted Stevie into Colin's ear. Colin nodded and smiled, and they both dropped another Rainbow Brite each. It was just after that that the first pills that they had taken started to hit them, properly, like a runaway train. *WHOOOOOOSH!*

Both were soon on the dancefloor giving it laldy, as Trevor Reilly dropped 'Saltwater' by Chicane into his set – a new anthem featuring Chicane's perfect beats and a sample of an old Clannad song.

Open my eyes saltwater rain
Fol lol the doh fol the day
Oscail mo shúil in that way
Fol lol the doh fol the day

As the crowd chanted:
Here we, here we, here we fuckin' go
Here we, here we, here we fuckin' go

Within an hour or so, Stevie and Colin found themselves sitting in the chill-out area, chewing their own faces off whilst talking to three lassies who were through from Bellshill. The lassies had invited them back to a house party afterwards, but by then, the two lads were toiling.

If you've been out drinking, doing party drugs, and dancing all night on the Friday, it's never the same buzz if you go out the next night, too. Those weird clubbers who just drink bevvy can do it, and a few hardened pillheads can manage it fine, but for most people, although going clubbing for a second night in a row sounds like a good idea, it's actually a terrible idea. You can still have a good time but the physical and psychological toll is just too heavy for most mere mortals. At best, you'll go home early, at worst, you'll become a bit of a sweating, dribbling basket case. The music, the lights, the crowd noise, everything is amplified. Then there's the non-specific paranoia. A weird sense of dread which comes out of nowhere.

Stevie and Colin were at the bar. By now the second Es they had dropped had well and truly kicked in; they were sweating, gurning, slavering messes. As they opened their umpteenth bottles of water, they stood at the crossroads faced by many clubbers.

Should they party on, or go home for the sake of their sanity?

The lassies from Bellshill hadn't been out the night before and had given every indication that their weekend was only just beginning. As much as they wanted to hang out with those three Lanarkshire goddesses a bit more, Colin and Stevie knew that to continue well into Sunday was a recipe for disaster and a Monday off sick from work, with all the headfuck shite that brought. Tired, sweating, paranoid, and feeling like a pair of zombies, they made do with getting a phone number from the lassies, promising to look them up during the week, then headed for the exit. It was 2am, where had the fucking time gone?

As they left the venue, a bouncer handed them a flyer for next week's event. Stevie asked for four flyers – he couldn't even read the text on them, but card flyers were always barrie for roach.

They were soon back in the car on the M8, heading east. Colin's blue firetrap shirt had a huge sweat rash down the back, while the back of Stevie's white jeans were manky, covered in wee spots of whatever that black slime is that you get on nightclub floors and walls. They looked like shit. They drove with the windows down, Stevie trying to build a joint on his lap in the passenger seat, as Colin drove, nervously checking the rear-view mirror every few minutes for the vast column of police cars that his paranoia assured him were following close behind. As they zoomed past the cinema at Coatbridge beside the M8, both let out big sighs of relief. They were almost home.

Going out again had been a huge mistake. Both agreed that they should've just had the dreaded 'quiet one' on that Saturday night and maybe looked in on Clare and Kirsty on the Sunday. They phoned Kirsty's house from the payphone at Harthill services when they stopped to get petrol, skins, more water and a couple of sandwiches that there was no fucking chance of either of them being able to eat in a million years.

Kirsty, aghast, couldn't believe that they had both went out AGAIN. She sounded like death warmed up and told them to come round in the afternoon, as Clare was coming round to watch football at hers. They could all chill, have a smoke, and maybe have a pizza or something.

That suited Colin and Stevie fine. In their minds, sex and romance on a Sunday afternoon with two witty, fun, gorgeous women would see them both nicely into the new week – assuming of course, that the lassies actually intended to shag them.

That left a gap of almost eight hours to fill for the lads, though. They were both melted, exhausted and, well, a fucking disgrace. Hitting somebody else's hoose back home for a party was an option, but it was their last resort option, as, like the club, two nights in a row of that can be draining, depressing even. Neither of them wanted any more class As. As they both lived with their parents, going home to chill out wasn't an option, dealing with family members when oot yer nut is a huge no-no.

Colin spoke as they neared the Whitburn junction on the Motorway.

'Here, man, why don't we head up the Bathgate Hills and have a few joints? I need to clear ma heid somewhere peaceful before goin' hame.'

'Aye, sound,' said Stevie. 'Maybe the fresh air will straighten us up,' he added.

Wishful thinking. It would take a session of electric-shock treatment to sober these two up.

Nevertheless, they left the motorway and headed for Beecraigs Country Park. As the white Peugeot 205 zoomed up and through the Bathgate Hills, the darkness of the night outside made it seems like they were travelling through space. Stevie put a Faithless CD on, and as the classic anthem, 'The Long Way Home', drew to an end, the car came to a halt in the eerie blackness of the country park's deserted car park.

I got it sleeping rough on the streets in the rain
I got it learning to share my people's pain
I got it making flowers grow in hearts of stone
I got it cos I always take the long way home

They both got out of the car, and Stevie sparked up the joint that he had seemed to take an entire millennium to roll. They'd both been too para to smoke it while driving. With their joint, some fags, a quarter of soap bar and their bottles of water, they headed for the picnic area.

Chapter Four

The Awakening

It wasn't uncommon back then to bump into other stray clubbers up there late at night or early in the morning. You could usually only see the lit ends of their fags or joints, though, so you had no idea who it was amid the dark, infinite night. On this night, there appeared to be nobody else around. The silence was so intense that it had a calming effect on both of them, chilling them out and, with the joint they were smoking, taking the edge off those bloody Rainbow Brite eccies.

Stevie was soon rolling another one, using the bench he was sitting on as a rolling table. Beecraigs is a heavily wooded country park where things like orienteering and nature rambling happen. There's an adventure playground for kids and even a small pond. The rest of it is just a series of well-trodden tracks through a mixture of evergreen and deciduous trees. There's also a really cool iron-age site nearby, popular with hippies and local geeks.

They were both melted and exhausted, and the cool breeze they had both enjoyed at first was now starting to feel more like an icy chill. It took them both a good 15 minutes to smoke the enormous 5-skinner number that Stevie had built, both of them taking turns to cough and splutter as if they were World War I mustard gas victims, but the weed also did its intended job – mellowing the pair. Colin was finishing off the joint, coughing as the burning reached the roach, when all of a sudden, out of nowhere, a booming voice behind them spoke.

'Are ye no' passing that? Greedy basturts!'

They both totally shat it and spun around to see who had spoken. There was nobody else around.

Then, right in front of their eyes, in the bark of the trunk of a large beech tree a few yards from the picnic area, a face appeared, with a carved wooden mouth and nose, and a pair of bright red eyes.

Colin and Stevie stared at each other in disbelief then looked again upon this bizarre apparition, open-mouthed, aghast. Colin dropped the smouldering roach on the grass beside the path.

'Hoggin' basturt,' boomed the voice from the tree. *'Get another wan rolled,'* it added.

A talking fucking tree!

The tree trunk shone in the darkness and a fiery red glow could be seen inside its mouth. Its eyes, too, were alight with a kind of flame. The face on the tree-trunk looked both magnificent and terrifying, weather-beaten and distinguished – features which kind of belied the deep, booming echoing yet also Weegie neddish voice that had emanated from within.

The two lads, disbelieving, looked at each other again then turned in unison to race back to the car.

'Haw, you two stay right where ye are,' boomed the tree after them. They both stopped running when they saw Colin's Peugeot 205 start to glow red, as if it were burning.

'I'll burn yer motor, do ye want me to burn yer motor? Ah'll fuckin' dae it! Ah will! Come back here!' said the tree.

They both turned around and walked back to where they had been standing. The glowing coming from the tree lit up the immediate area around them, attracting many flying insects, which annoyed both of them and the tree.

'*Fuck's sake, I hate these fuckin' things ... AAAACHOOO!*'

The tree's nose wiggled, and it sneezed loudly, which seemed to scare off the majority of the flying pests. Colin looked back to the car, and to his relief, it seemed to be okay; the glowing had stopped.

'*Yer motor's fine, Colin. Right, youze two, what the fuck are ye daein' up here at this time? Are yez poofters?*'

Colin turned to Stevie again, who shrugged and just said, 'Better answer him, mate.'

Colin said, 'Naw, we're no' gay, he's ma best mate. This is Stevie and I'm...'

'*Ah ken yer fuckin' names, Stevie and Colin, a couple of pillheads by the look of it, ye probably came up here to clear yer heids after a heavy weekend, am I right?*' boomed the tree in a slightly friendlier, yet still intimidating tone.

'Aye, that's us. How do ye ken that?' replied Colin, nervously.

'*Ah ken everything. In case yez were wonderin', I'm a wood fairy. Ah ken everything. I'm all powerful and all knowing. Ask us anything, go on, ask us anything.*'

'What, anything?' asked Colin.

'*Aye, anything,*' said the tree, confidently.

'Anything at all?' asked Stevie.

'*Aye, fire away. Ask and you shall be telt,*' boomed the tree, smugly.

'So, are you gonnae grant us three wishes?' Colin asked.

'*Ah'm Ah fuck. Dae Ah look like a fuckin' magic lamp? You think Ah've goat a genie waiting in ma jaxie? Next question, please, ya cunt.*'

Stevie added, 'Awright, awright awright, who's gonnae win the fitba the morn, then? I mean, today.'

'*Dinnae ken that wan,*' boomed the tree, deadpan.

Colin and Stevie looked at each other again.

'*Haw, I'm an all-powerful wood fairy, no' fuckin' Mystic Meg, Ah'm no' here to give you betting tips. Ask me something else, go on,*' growled the tree, then it mumbled to itself, and shoogled its face as if shaking its head in exasperation. '*The knowledge of the Earth at my beck and call and they're asking me for a fuckin' fitba score, jeez, this is gonnae be a long night.*'

'Awright then, what have we been up tae this weekend, then?' asked Stevie.

'*Yez were at a gay bar,*' boomed the tree.

Before Colin or Stevie could answer the tree continued.

'*Ach, Ah'm only kiddin'. Ye were at that room at the top place in Bathgate wi' aw yer pals on Friday night, ye aw got melted, ye were at a decent party in Longridge– which, I might add, isn't something that has happened there very often in history. Then yez went back wi' a couple of tidy birds fae the scheme to chill, but circumstances beyond your control meant that naebody got laid. You then, to postpone your inevitable comedown, foolishly went through to The Arches in Glasgow last night, where you over-indulged in they new Rainbow Brite eccies, danced like a pair of zombies with cattle prods rammed up their arses, totally blew it wi' three tidy lassies fae Bellshill, and now here you are, up the fuckin' woods, pondering your existence, seeking serenity, and, well, aw that pish. Oh, and ye stopped at Harthill on the way back to get skins and to phone one ae they birds. Am I impressing you yet? Later today you're meeting up wi' those two lassies fae Friday night again to watch the fitba and chill. Am I right?*'

The tree's facial expression changed to a slightly more cheerful one, it took pride in its soothsaying, it seemed.

Colin and Stevie stood open-mouthed and didn't need to answer.

'*See, Ah ken everything. Ah'm an all-powerful wood fairy,*' boomed the tree, then its tone of voice became slightly warmer. '*Look, ehh, lads, I realise this must be a bit of a shock. Stevie, why don't you build a joint on that bench there and we can all have a chat.*'

Stevie, his mind blown yet still accepting the situation, began to do just that. The tree continued, turning its attention to Colin.

'*Right, you, get the beer oot. Ah'd love a cauld yin.*'

'We've no' got any drink, mate, just a few bottles of water, do ye want some water?'

'*Ah'm a fuckin' tree. Ah sit here aw day every day in the pishing rain, and when it's no' rainin' Ah've goat animals pishin' on me. Naw I dinnae want any fuckin' water. Ya fuckin' teapot. For fuck's sake. You, Stevie, how's that joint progressing, Ah'm gaspin',*' ranted the tree.

'I'm just burning weed in now, winnae be long…'

'*Burning weed in? What, soap bar? Christ, you're a right pair of amateurs are ye no'? Never heard of grass?*'

'That's all we've got, mate, grass is hard to get, eh,' replied Stevie, slightly annoyed at having the quality of his soap bar impugned. 'So, yer no' wanting any, then?' he added, cheekily.

'*Ah never fuckin' said that,*' snapped the tree. '*Get a move on. teapot,*' it added. Stevie continued rolling.

As Stevie rolled, Colin stood, still aghast, yet, like Stevie, he had quickly accepted the absurd reality of their current situation.

'*That's a belter of a sweat rash on yer back, Colin, I bet you were the belle of the ball wi' that. Still, no' as daft as yer mate's white jeans. Who the fuck still wears white jeans?*' said the tree, in a mocking tone. Its eyes swivelled around a bit, seeming to be scanning the surrounding area. Then, the tree gave a sigh, and its tone became friendlier. '*So, Friday was a big one for you guys, eh? What's the Room at the Top like?*'

'Aye it was a good night, we were aw melted, it was just the regular resident DJs, but we prefer that. Have you been?' Colin asked.

'How the fuck would I have been there? Do you see many enchanted beech trees cutting shapes on the dancefloor in places like that? Are you dense, son?'

'Naw, jeezo, sorry mate, just making conversation, keep yer canopy on.'

The tree's face twisted into what seemed like pure rage, but then it let out a jovial, though still menacing, belly laugh. The tree laughed so hard that tears began to roll down its face. The laughter echoed all around the woods, filling the night air. It seemed to calm Colin and Stevie a little. Stevie was now standing next to Colin and was invoking roller's rights: smoking the freshly rolled joint. The aroma of soap bar and tobacco filled the air.

'Keep ma canopy on, that's a good one, son. Listen, I've no' laughed like that in years. It's usually hard to strike up any sort of witty banter wi' folk when ye've just scared the shite oot of them in a forest during the night. They usually scream and just run away. I like you two, maybe yer no' the bawbags I took ye for. Eh ... Stevie, passin' that?'

Stevie saw that the tree, which now had eyebrows, had raised them and appeared to be waiting for something. Nervously, he approached. The Tree's eyes remained fixed on him. Stevie asked the tree how he'd like the joint.

'Hold it up tae ma mooth and I'll dae the rest,' said the tree, excitedly.

Stevie held the roach end of the joint up to the tree's mouth, and the tree began to suck in the smoke. Its mouth was so big that this caused a little breeze to circulate around them all, which was welcome to the two lads who were sweating and rough, still, yet also fascinated. As the tree inhaled more and more, the fiery red glow inside of it grew stronger, lighting up the area even more. It had inhaled more than half of the joint before Stevie pulled it away, stepped back, and handed the remainder of it to Colin, who took his turn.

The tree began to cough and splutter loudly; in between the coughs and splutters which shook the ground and nearby trees, it mumbled something about 'fuckin' soap bar', and coughed some more. Then it stopped coughing, and seemed to exhale, blowing weed smoke all over Colin and Stevie, who were still transfixed. When the tree had finished exhaling, it gave an 'ahhhhhh' of relief, blinked a few times, then smiled. Its big eyes were now wide and bloodshot, with heavy lids. Its face seemed to have relaxed, too, and each corner of its mouth curled upwards, giving the tree's previously twisted and contorted face a far more chilled look.

'Fuck me, that's better, lads, thank you. Here, that soap bar's actually no' bad,' said the tree, with a slower, more friendly, yet still booming tone.

Stevie and Colin were muttering amongst themselves for a moment while the tree sat at rest, staring vacantly into space for a time.

'I'm no' askin' him, you ask him,' said Colin.

'Aye, awright then,' said Stevie. I'll build the joints, I'll score the eccies, I'll try to break the ice wi' the fucking enchanted tree monster...'

'Ah'm a fuckin' wood fairy, son, get it right,' said the tree, giggling.

Colin and Stevie started to giggle, too, then they laughed, and the tree laughed, all three of them laughed out loud, as the cannabis took effect. Stevie continued.

'So, eh, what's yer name, mate?' asked Stevie, adding 'and, eh...what's the deal wi' you being up here, in the woods, like?'

Though its voiced still echoed loudly, the tree sounded far calmer now, sedate even.

'My name is Sandy – and aye, I'm a beech tree so ye might say Ah'm a sandy beech. But if ye dae say that, I'll change my mind aboot burnin' yer motor. But, I suppose an explanation is in order.'

The two lads sat down on the grass in front of the tree, as it began to tell them a most curious tale.

Chapter Five

House Arrest

Back in 1989, Sandy had been down at a big acid house party at The Hacienda in Manchester. At an after-party in Salford, he and three friends had overindulged in magic mushrooms, then decided to go for a drive. They managed to drive all the way to Glasgow, where at another house party they had met some hippies from Edinburgh. The plan had been to follow the hippies through to a secret illegal outdoor rave at Edinburgh's Blackford quarry, but the police followed their three-vehicle convoy all the way from Glasgow to Bathgate along the M8, inducing paranoia in all travelling, as they carried with them around 30 doves, some pink champagne speed, some Quaaludes and two large bags of grass – enough back then for *intent to supply* and a near fuckin' life-sentence in the jail. Sandy and his mates had come off the M8 at Bathgate to escape, hoping the cops would stay on the motorway but the polis had chosen to follow them. Luckily for them, Sandy and his mates were in a Sierra RS Cosworth and were able to outrun and evade the police, soon finding themselves driving blindly in the Bathgate Hills. They stopped and got out of the car when they reached what looked like some old iron-age site, which amazed them. Still tripping their nuts off, they lost track of time and remained at Cairnpapple all day, doing spinny dances and chanting nonsense on the ancient, circular stone curiosity, from where they could see for many miles in every direction. On the way back down from Cairnpapple, another police car had appeared behind them and turned on its siren. Rather than risk a deadly high-speed race on country roads they didn't know, Sandy and his friends; Leanne, Charlotte, and Blair, had abandoned the car and run off into the countryside in three different directions, so that the police couldn't chase them all. Standard operating procedure for weekend druggies at the time. Sandy suspected that the police had tailed them because of an informant – the chase had been too much of a coincidence.

Sandy had run and run, he didn't know how long for, but he ended up in Beecraigs Country Park.

He had stopped to rest for a while at a picnic area, but a police car had loomed into view in the distance. He was trapped. A young woman with long black hair and a pretty face, who appeared to be hillwalking in the area, had sort of appeared from the trees and said hello. Sandy had frantically asked her what way he could run, and the woman had assured him she knew where he could hide. She knew all the paths, she knew everything, she said. Sandy followed her over to a large beech tree, then the woman again assured him that she knew everything. Then, she asked Sandy if he wanted to know everything, too, to which he replied that he did. Then she made him say, 'I want to know everything'. Time was of the essence, so when she asked him to say it again, he did. Sandy could now see the police through the trees, on foot, still some distance away but heading in their direction. The sexy young woman, smiling, her eyes dark pool of lust, took off her blue Berghaus jacket. Sandy noticed that she had huge breasts, straining at her tight, thin Benetton tee-shirt. She was beautiful, magically so, almost seeming to glow with sexuality – he wanted her, but now wasn't the time or the place for any of that – or maybe it was?

Then, she reached out and stroked the side of Sandy's face with her manicured fingers, and winked, still smiling, asking him to say it one more time, then she would help him escape.

'I want to know everything,' Sandy had said. The woman had immediately begun to laugh maniacally, scornfully, then she disappeared into thin air, right before his very eyes. The police were getting close. Sandy, shocked, still tripping, just stood still. To his considerable surprise, the cops walked right past him, as if he wasn't there. Sandy felt stuck; he couldn't bring himself to run. How had they not seen him? Two minutes later, the cops walked by again. It was getting dark, and they still didn't see him. Sandy had waited until he heard their car depart, crunching its wheels on the gravel track. It was only then, when he tried to leave the scene of this extraordinary encounter, that he couldn't. He was rooted to the spot. The beech tree was gone.

Except, it wasn't.

Sandy *was* the tree, now.

Colin and Stevie looked like wide-eyed schoolchildren as the tree recounted this tale, Stevie even rolled another joint and took it straight to the tree, giving it another long toke, making it glow again. As it then exhaled, the tree concluded its tale.

'She wiznae a hillwalker, she was a wood fairy. She'd been trapped in the tree, and the only way that she could get out was to find some stupid gullible tosser, like me, and make him say 'I want to know everything', three times. Years later, a wise owl told me that's what wood fairies dae. They're cunts, man. Now I'm a wood fairy, stuck in this fuckin' tree for eternity, well, unless I can convince some other daft cunt to say the mantra to me three times. Worse still, I only get a chance to do that once every five years. It was the owl who filled me in on the basics, he was sound, until some wee bastards wi' an air rifle done him in last year. So, that's me, all powerful, within this glade, all

knowing, but the knowledge does me no good. I can only appear and speak to people at night. as you can imagine, the last ten years have been murder. Whenever I do get the chance to talk to any cunt, it's nearly always some roaster like youze, oot their nut, or they bloody doggers who come up here on a Thursday night.'

Stevie started sniggering, but the tree snapped at him.

'It's no' bloody funny.'

'Sorry, mate,' said Stevie.

'In 1994, five years after it first happened, I nearly had some daftie who was melted after a Rezerection rave saying the mantra three times. I appeared in front of him as a female forest ranger, jeez, I was tidy, but the wee scrote took a whitey after saying it twice and then his mates shouted on him, and bang, I'm back to being a fuckin' tree again.

'It's no' aw bad, mind. Often, for kicks, I appear to solitary ramblers, stray clubbers, and the like and give them a bit of a show, make my bark glow, make daft noises at them, sometimes even engage them in chat, but I only do that to weirdos: freakish people whom nobody would believe if they told folk they met a talking tree up the woods. There's probably folk in Carstairs or the Royal Ed because of me. So, lads, what do you make of that?'

Colin said, 'It's 1999 now, five years on from '94, you're due another chance of escape. You're no' gonnae try to trap one of us, are ye, mate?'

'Naw,' said the tree. 'Are you fuckin' dense? I wouldn't have telt ye that whole story, including the bit about the mantra, if that was my intention, would I? Fuckin' teapot!'

Stevie said, 'Wow, that's some story, mate. Ah'm sorry that's happened to ye. Is there no' anybody who can cast a spell or something to set you free, without trapping anybody else? Like, a wizard, or something?'

'A wizard? A fuckin' wizard? Gandalf perhaps? Ye think this is Lord of the Rings or some other magical realm oot a book or a cartoon? Daftie!'

'Ok, ok, sorry mate, only trying to help.'

'Truth is, fuck knows. It's no' like I had an induction day after that cow forcibly recruited me to the wood fairy fraternity, is it? There's nae instruction manual either. If there is any other way out, Ah ken fuck all aboot it, all I ken is that Ah'm stuck in this fuckin' tree. If they wee bastards wi' the Webley .22 hadn't killed my owl mate, perhaps I'd ken mare, but I dinnae. Lads, that's the sun aboot to come up, I'll be leaving you shortly.'

Colin and Stevie rose to their feet. Colin spoke. 'Well mate, it's been sound meeting ye, will you be alright? Want us to look in on ye again next week?'

'Aye, sound, and bring some decent weed and some beer next time. go on, fuck off. Roasters. Catch ye, ciao.'

The tree's face faded and vanished as the first shafts of the early morning sunrise began to flood the country park. Colin and Stevie shrugged their shoulders and headed back to the car, birdsong in the air. They got to the car, rolled another joint, then drove back to the scheme, after all, magic enchanted tree or no, they had a date to keep with Kirsty and Clare soon, and a football match to watch.

Chapter Six

Cry

Later that day, the two lads turned up at Kirsty's, a little the worse for wear, but both had showered and changed. They watched the football with Kirsty and had some cans and a few joints. Rangers beat Celtic 3–0 at Parkhead, to win the league. Colin was nominally a Celtic fan, Stevie was Rangers, but as both were true ravers who abhorred sectarianism as being the antithesis of dance music culture, they enjoyed the match but with no more joy or enthusiasm than if they had watched a decent movie – at least they could all talk about the match with work colleagues during the week. That was about as far as both of their interests in football went.

Clare wasn't there. Kirsty, who still seemed a bit rough from the weekend's exploits too, had told them that Clare's ex, a local psychopath named Kerr, had followed her home from her shift at the pub the previous evening and had tried to force entry into Clare's home, steaming drunk, demanding she get back with him. Kerr was in his late 30s and was not to be messed with. He and Clare had actually been finished for over a year, but, every few weeks, something like this would happen. Kirsty told the lads that usually Clare gave as good as she got, and if she couldn't get rid of Kerr herself, she usually just phoned the police, who would come and lift him – but never charged him. Something about last night's stalking incident had freaked Clare out, though, so she had gone to East Calder, to stay with her parents for a few nights. Kirsty said that Kerr had threatened to put Clare in hospital – something that had been his MO with women for years.

Kirsty didn't have Clare's mum's house number, so, none of them could phone her. All three were worried about her. That Kerr was a bastard – a real bastard.

So, the cosy Sunday that Colin and Stevie had planned didn't really pan out the way that they had hoped. They were all a bit deflated by the Clare news. Colin went home in the early evening, having no desire to cock-block his best mate. He stumbled home and slept like the dead until work on the Monday morning. Stevie and Kirsty later fucked like a pair of horny rabbits for a while on the sofa, then fell asleep in each other's arms, exhausted, relieved, warm, and content, their postponed passion and desire from Friday night finally sated. It had been worth the wait.

At no time that Sunday, did Colin or Stevie mention anything to Kirsty about a talking tree.

Monday evening saw the two lads sitting in their local scheme pub, *The Castle,* ostensibly to watch the Monday night SKY English premiership match, but actually to try for a few pints to help soothe the mental wreckage in their heads from the weekend. The pub was quite busy, always was on a Monday. Nobody in the place really gave a toss about Arsenal V Derby County blaring on the pub's new gigantic 32-inch telly in the corner.

Colin was still wearing his navy-blue warehouse overalls and looked gaunt, his head pishing with sweat. Stevie had been home to change and was wearing stonewashed jeans and a blue sweater, the back of which was stencilled in fancy white letters *'100% Pure Chevignon'.* This cringeworthy item of clothing had been bought from his mum's catalogue but had quickly been relegated to 'at home or local pub use only' – as was evident by the large hot-rock burns down the front.

They were both still rough as fuck, but Tennent's lager would hopefully numb that – the Monday night sleep is always the best after a mental weekend.

Colin said, 'Mate, that was mental up at Beecraigs, did that really happen or have I been trippin'?'

Stevie looked around the bar and, satisfied that nobody was listening, glugged some more lager then answered.

'Aye. It happened. There's things in this world that nobody can explain, man. I'm glad you mentioned it cos for a while today I convinced myself that they Rainbow Brite eccies had made me imagine it all. Poor Sandy, trapped in that tree aw they years. Life's a bitch, eh?'

'Don't ye think it's a bit weird that both of us seem so no' freaked out by this?'

'A bit, aye. Then again, it was more real than any of that Jesus stuff we got at the school, eh? Or they crop circles we saw on the Discovery channel.'

Colin shook his head, laughed, and took another drink from his pint. A dull cheer erupted in the bar as Nicholas Anelka scored for Arsenal. Again.

Then, the pub door swung open and in walked Kirsty, still wearing her work uniform from the supermarket. Her blonde hair was tied up and the frumpy blouse and cargo trousers she wore did their best to hide her shapely figure. Oddly, Kirsty walked straight past the two lads and made for the bar, ordering two long vodkas. She was already downing the second one by the time Colin and Stevie had joined her at the bar.

'Is everything awright, Kirsty?' Stevie asked.

They could both see that Kirsty had been crying and was on the edge of something. She had red marks on her neck and wrists. As she finished downing the second long-vodka and ordered a third, Stevie asked again, 'What's happened, Kirsty? Tell us.'

'No' here', answered Kirsty, nodding her head towards an empty booth at the far end of the pub, where the three of them went and sat down.

'What's happened?' asked Colin.

Kirsty was silent for a moment then said 'Kerr. That bastard Kerr.'

Gavin Kerr, Clare's ex, wasn't just a bastard – he was more like *the* bastard. And he was a cunt, too.

He was the main hash dealer in the scheme, he also sold speed and there were rumours that he sold heroin, through a lackey, too. He was a skinhead, short at five foot eight but stocky, and a fucking animal in a fight. In addition to selling drugs, he also ran a protection racquet on certain vulnerable local businesses throughout the town and owned a tanning salon in the shopping centre, which he used to launder money. He'd done bits and bobs of jail time throughout his infamous career, but nothing like the time he deserved. Amazingly, he'd never been collared for anything to do with his illegal business activities, only for assaults and GBH. Back in 1994, he had broken a guy's legs over a £200 tick bill, but the procurator fiscal had made a right arse of the case and Kerr had walked away from that one. Then, in 1996, his victim, a young lad named Danny who would never have said 'boo' to a goose, had died from a blood clot, quite probably caused by the fucked-up circulation in his legs which Kerr's beating had caused.

Kirsty related a tale of woe. She had arrived home from work that day and had just put her key in the lock when Kerr had appeared behind her, startling her. He'd been friendly at first and Kirsty had chosen to let him in for a coffee, knowing he was there to fish for information about his ex, Clare, but Kirsty was sure she could placate the nutter and send him on his way, without letting slip where Clare was.

'I don't know' wasn't the answer Kerr wanted to hear. He had exploded with rage, throwing his full coffee cup at the wall, narrowly missing the TV, leaving coffee splattered everywhere. Kirsty had tried to go for the phone, but he had grabbed her forearms and held them above her head, hurting her, asking again for Clare's whereabouts.

'Ah dinnae ken. Kerr, yer hurtin' me,' pleaded Kirsty.

Kerr had let go of her arms then grabbed her around the throat, pushing her against the wall, roaring 'Tell me!'

Kirsty was crying. Kerr squeezed her throat firmly enough to cause distress but not so hard as to actually choke her – he was a dab hand at such things, as his numerous battered exes could doubtless testify. Kerr had then ranted menacingly.

'Ah know you ken where she is. Ah also know the pair of ye have been getting melted wi' they two wee pricks. Ah know everything. What wan is Clare shaggin'? Is it that Stevie or the other wan? I'll kill the pair ae them. Would ye like that, ya wee skank? Or maybe you and me could head through to your bedroom and I'll show ye what a real man can dae to ye? Would ye like that?'

Terrified, Kirsty just shook her head. Kerr seemed to then realise he had maybe gone a bit far and released his grip on Kirsty's neck. He then had the cheek to stroke the side of her face and turned to exit, but before he did, he left a parting shot, tapping the side of his head as if to say 'whoops, almost forgot'.

'Aw aye, if you see Clare before Ah dae, tell her that £500 she still owes me for gear is now £1500, and Ah want it by the end of the month, or she's fuckin' deed. Interest, know what I mean? And tell yer wee boyfriends Ah'm lookin' for them, they'd better hope Ah find Clare before Ah bump intae them, or they'll no' be daein' much dancing thereafter.' And with that, the drug-addled psychopath left the building, slamming the door on the way out. Kirsty had let out a huge sigh of relief, then rushed to the toilet to be sick. She had then sat on her sofa for an hour or so, shaking, unsure what to do, then, almost on autopilot, had headed for *The Castle*.

Colin and Stevie were angry, and frightened, upon hearing that sad tale. Kirsty cautioned them against any rash action.

Then, Colin spoke 'Fuck, this is heavy, what are we gonnae do?'

Chapter Seven

Lizard

Like all psychopathic drug dealers, Kerr was virtually bombproof in the schemes. He controlled the supply of drugs, and this also gave him unique access to information about almost everybody else in the scheme. Though a hardman himself, Kerr could also call upon an entourage of fellow scumbags and junkies to help him out when he either required muscle or sought to inflict violence or intimidation without getting his own hands dirty. He had a crew, but they weren't his *friends*, more like his minions. Some were guys and lassies who wanted the kudos that being pals with a gangster, and the protection that brought, would add to their own reputation in the scheme. Others were speed or coke addicts who courted his attention because they wanted to ensure a regular supply of drugs at slightly reduced *mate's rates*, or because they feared his wrath were they to start buying gear from one of his competitors. Most of Kerr's 'friends' owed him money, or a favour, or both, and Kerr used it as leverage whenever he needed anything from them, or, if he just felt like bamming them up for kicks.

He did have one true friend, or at least something close to it. Fat Carson, real name, William Carson Forbes. They had been joined at the hip since school. Carson was very much in the low 20s IQ-wise, but he was six foot four and had the physique of a grizzly bear. He was the closest thing Kerr had to a right-hand man. Carson usually accompanied Kerr on debt-collecting trips and when he wasn't breaking the bones of working-class debtors he could usually be found at Kerr's infamous drugs and hookers parties, usually laughing at, or agreeing with, everything Kerr said. Kerr was Dastardly, Carson was Muttley. To reckon with Kerr, you had to reckon with Fat Carson.

Kerr himself didn't even live in the scheme, he lived in a huge bungalow in a private development on the fringes of town, bought with all the money he'd rinsed from the poor sods in the scheme over the years. Whatever the Tories hadn't taken from the working-class people in the scheme, Kerr hoovered up – that's neoliberalism in its purest form, innit?

Deranged gangsters like Kerr usually operate by some sort of fucked-up moral code. His was very short. Having grown up in the schemes himself, he never bothered any of his customers' parents – he wouldn't go to somebody's door if they lived with their mum and dad. He took great pity on the sick and disabled – unless they owed him money, and the main rule was that he never did anything bad to law-abiding ordinary folk or businesses who were nothing to do with the drugs or crime scene, and he didn't operate in the town's more upmarket 'bought house' areas. Of course, this moral code of his also, handily, meant that the police had absolutely fuck-all interest in his activities – as far as they were concerned, it was all merely scum-on-scum. The authorities didn't even bat an eyelid at his huge house and flashy car, despite his only registered business being *Tan and go*, his tanning salon and glaringly obvious money laundering front, for which, of course, he always paid his taxes and suppliers on time. It was usually staffed by young women who owed him drug debt, though, usually the ones he didn't want to use for sex in lieu of payment, or the ones that he had already fucked then decided to enslave them in his salon, instead.

Kerr even had the brass neck to donate small amounts of his drugs earnings to local sports clubs and community groups. Most of the young men coaching the sports teams were doing so as part of a drug and alcohol recovery program, so in the twisted mind of men like Kerr, the £500 a year he donated to the local youth football club more than made up for the hundreds of thousands of pounds he took each year from the poor working-class punters in the schemes. Kind of like Jimmy Savile and his marathons.

Chapter Eight

Castles in the Sky

Now back at Kirsty's place, away from prying ears, Colin, Stevie, and Kirsty were drinking a small pub-bought carry-out – *SKOL Lager, bleurgh* – and having a few joints while they talked about how best to help Clare and deal with that bastard Kerr.

Stevie mooted the idea of giving Kerr a beating with baseball bats. This suggestion made Kirsty laugh, but she apologised.

'Naw, sorry, but ... you two giving him a doing? I dinnae think so. Maybe if you got him alone, you'd have a chance, but that Fat Carson or his other minions are usually at his house, they'd fuckin' kill ye. Even without them being there, nae offence lads, but Kerr's mad, he'd probably do the two of you in himself and shove the chibs up yer arses – and then he'd make the rest of our lives a misery, AND he'd give Clare even more hassle, too. Naw, that's no' an option. Besides, even if you done him in, he'd be back. You'd have to leave town, forever. So, naw, we're no' daein' that. We'd have to kill him, for that to work, and I dinnae think any of us fancy a 30-stretch for that cunt, do we?'

'What aboot grassing him in?' Colin suggested.

Stevie and Kirsty both let out long breaths, loudly, at that situation. 'That's an option,' said Stevie.

Kirsty, shaking her head, said, 'Grass him for what? The polis ken aw aboot his activities, they dinnae care. If rumour is true and he has polis as customers tae, they'll just tell him. Then we'll be outed as grasses. *If* we were guaranteed to get him banged up it might be worth a try, but even if they managed to get him on the dealing, he'll still be in the scheme for months before court. He'll still be free, free to slash us to bits for grassin' him, fuck that.'

Nobody in a scheme wants to be a grass. It's the only thing as low as a being a beast. Funny that, eh? How violent thuggery and thievery are somehow above those two things. So goes the scheme.

There was a moment's silence as all three of them racked their brains. 'Music sounds better with you' by Stardust was playing on the hi-fi.

Ooh baby I feel like
The music sounds better with you
Love might
Bring us both together

'Well, Batman and Robin, any more ideas?' Kirsty asked.

As if telepathically, Stevie and Colin looked at each other. Stevie nodded to Colin. Colin spoke.

'Err, Kirsty, we ken somebody who might be able tae help...'

'Naw, there's nae point trying to get any of your daft rave mates to do him in, either, besides, even if they're able, he'll ken it was us, he's fond of reminding folk he kens everything...'

'Naw, no' that for fuck's sake,' answered Colin. 'You tell her,' he snapped at Stevie. Stevie sighed and spoke.

'Look, Kirsty, we might have a way to sort this, but we'll need you to promise you'll believe us and no' think we're fuckin' radio rental.'

'Aye, ok, tell me who it is,' said Kirsty.

Stevie looked at Colin, then spoke to Kirsty again.

'Let's go for a wee drive to Beecraigs. We'll explain it aw on the way.'

'Beecraigs, whit the fuck are we gawn up there for?' asked Kirsty.

Soon, all three of them were in Colin's white Peugeot 205, heading for the Bathgate Hills.

'Hahahaha youze are aff yer fuckin' rocker!'

Kirsty was hee-hawing with laughter as the car climbed further up into the Bathgate Hills, on that dark night.

'A talking tree? Youze need tae lay aff they eccies. So, you met a talking magic tree, it smokes hash and it's gonnae help us?' Scoffed Kirsty, her voice a mix of derision, delirious laughter, and disbelief.

Since Stevie and Kirsty were the ones shagging each other, Stevie thought he'd best answer.

'Kirsty, c'mon, you promised you'd believe us. It's a wood fairy, by the way, no' a magic tree. A promise is a promise.'

Stevie, sprawled out in the back seat, had noted that Kirsty, in the front passenger seat looked just as hot in her work stuff as she did in her clubbing gear. He wondered if he was falling for her and he felt excited every time he caught her checking him out via the car's mirrors, which she wasn't very discrete about. Guys like that – a woman who knows what she wants.

Kirsty reached forward and skipped the CD track from the superb but noisy Fatboy Slim remix of Cornershop's 'Brimfull of Asha', to the cheesy but still brilliant 'Mysterious Times' by Sash!, which, given the trio's current situation, seemed apt. The wee white car neared Beecraigs, with the tunes pumpin'.

Real
Nothing is real
In a world of illusion, you only see what you feel
And we're feeling a change, and we don't know why
Choose one direction just one for a time
Don't say I'm thinking too much if you see what's behind
And these are mysterious times

It had actually taken more than just a promise to hold Kirsty to coming up to Beecraigs to meet this talking tree. Stevie had bet her the last two of those Rainbow Brite eccies, left over from The Arches, that they were telling the truth, and Kirsty had accepted the bet.

The car pulled into the car park in Beecraigs Country Park and came to a halt, the music stopping as the car stopped. With Colin driving, Stevie had built three joints in record time en route and they had also brought along a few cans of the mingin' pisswater SKOL Lager.

Kirsty swiped one of the joints and sparked it up as soon as they were out of the car and all trudging over to the picnic area, near the big beech tree. It was pitch black, there was no wind, and the only sound to be heard was their own footsteps on the track. They came to a halt beside the tree.

Colin placed the four cans of SKOL on the ground in front of the tree.

'Right, Kirsty, try no' tae freak oot too much, this dude kens us. Dinnae be scared.'

Kirsty said nothing, but she passed the joint to Stevie, and the three of them stood before the tree, nervous, excited, and fascinated.

The tree didn't move and hadn't shown its face yet. There was a minute of silence, before Stevie spoke.

'Mate, it's us, remember us? Stevie and Colin? We bring gifts, look, beer, and here, a joint for ye. This is our pal, Kirsty.'

Nothing. All they saw was a beech tree, barely illuminated by moonlight and the smoking end of their fat joint.

Colin spoke.

'Mate, c'mon it's us, wake up, we need to talk to ye. C'mon man. Want a beer?'

Still, nothing, just an ordinary tree.

They finished that first joint and waited for what seemed like an eternity. Nothing.

'Youze two need fuckin' help. Ah cannae believe I fell for this. Are you sure it wiznae acid you were on last time you were up here? A talking tree! Hahaha. Stevie, you owe me two eccies.'

Kirsty seemed a bit annoyed, but Stevie was kinda glad she seemed to have chilled out since her frightening brush with Kerr, earlier. Stevie reached into the wee Johnny pocket of his stonewashed jeans and fished out the two pink 'n' white speckled Rainbow Brites, handing them to Kirsty, who immediately put them inside her bra.

'Ah'm gawn back to wait in the car, I'll leave you two loonies here to talk tae yer fuckin' imaginary friend, thanks for the eccies, by the way,' laughed Kirsty, as she turned and headed back to the car. Colin spoke when she was out of earshot.

'Stevie, mate, maybe we did imagine that whole thing wi' the tree, they pills were really strong. We were wasted.' Colin sparked up the second big joint.

'Aye, maybe you're right, mate, but how could we both have tripped the same thing? Ah well, what the fuck are we gonnae dae aboot this Kerr cunt, now?' Then he added, 'Geez a draw ae that joint, then let's get back hame.'

'*Hoggin' basturts,*' boomed a familiar voice. '*Geez that.*'

The voice wasn't as loud as it had been the first time.

Colin and Stevie saw that face appear in the tree trunk in front of them again. The gnarled, distinguished, magnificent, scary yet also strangely shifty looking face. Its eyes and mouth only glowed faintly, this time. It blinked a few times.

'Well? Where's ma fuckin' joint? Ah'm chokin' here,' said the tree. It was obviously keeping its voice low and barely glowing, so that Kirsty wouldn't notice it from the car.

Colin walked over and held the fat five-skinner joint up to the tree's mouth. It took a long puff, held it in, spluttered slightly, then exhaled, the cloud of smoke it expelled temporarily enveloping Stevie and Colin. Stevie spoke.

'What was that aw aboot, mate? Could ye no' hear us?'

'Aye, Ah could fuckin' hear and see ye, mind Ah'm a wood fairy, all knowing, all seeing, aw that pish.'

'Then why would ye no' appear when Kirsty was here?' asked Stevie.

'Because Ah'm a wood fairy, and wood fairies are cunts, mind I telt ye that last time? No' ma fault if ye dinnae fuckin' listen, is it?'

Colin said, 'We brought you a smoke and some beer, man, thought you'd like that'

'Geez the fuckin' beer, now. Come on, get a fuckin' move on,' said the tree, a sense of urgency in its voice.

Colin clicked open a can of SKOL and held the can up to the tree's mouth, gently pouring in the beer. A gurgling noise omitted from the inside of the tree and some beer missed its mouth and dribbled down the bark at the sides. When the can was finished, Colin stepped backwards to stand beside Stevie again.

The tree burped and hiccupped a few times, but then let out an audible '*aaaaahhhhh*', smacking its lips, then its face seemed to rest. Its eyes were now heavy from the joint, too.

'*That's ma first drink since 1989, lads, oh boy, that's taken the edge aff. Geez another wan...*'

Colin picked up another can, but Stevie reached his arm out to stop him, then spoke to the stoned tree.

'Mate, we've brought you beer and a smoke, like you asked, why did you no' appear when Kirsty was here, nae mare beer or joints until ye tell us! Right, Col?'

Colin was shocked at Stevie's bravado but answered 'Right. Nane.'

'*Ah'll burn yer fuckin' motor,*' threatened the tree, as he had the last time, but Stevie was having none of it. His blood was up.

'Ah dinnae gee a fuck. Burn it. The woman I think I love is sitting in that motor right now, if you touch that motor, I'll come back wi' a fuckin' chainsaw the morra and it's adios for you, pal, Mr know-it-aw wood fairy. And I'll dae it in daylight when you're powerless to stop me. Look, we've had a really heavy few days; Kirsty was threatened by some scumbag gangster today – same guy who says he's gonnae kill her pal, Clare, AND he's after us now, tae.'

'*Ah'm no' here to appear and disappear to cater to you cunts' every whim, to help you impress women, just so ye can get yer hole. No fuckin' danger. If ye want to impress a bird, take her up the toon or away tae Paris or something. Ah'm no' here just for your amusement, Ah'm no' your fuckin' sex aid, fuckin' teapots,*' said the tree, in a smug, condescending tone.

Stevie was really annoyed now.

'You're a dick, that's no' why we brought her up here; we brought her up here to prove that you exist and ...' Stevie hesitated for a second, '... tae ask for yer fuckin' help, dealing wi' this bullying gangster. Help us, man.'

The tree stood silent for what seemed like an eternity, rolled its eyes, sighed, then spoke.

'*Well, why didn't ye fuckin' say so? Ah fuckin' hate bullies. Mind, Ah was a raver before I was a wood fairy, one love, man. Ok ok ok, let's get her back over from the car. By the way, she's really tidy, Stevie, how did ye pull her? Rohypnol?*'

'Aye, very funny, I'll just go 'n' get her,'

'*Nae need,*' said the tree. It then fixed its eyes on the distant Peugeot 205 and its eyes began to glow red. The car's alarm suddenly went off, the doors and boot sprung open and all of the car's lights began to flash. A female voice cried out, 'WHAT THE FUCK' and, sure enough, Kirsty soon came bolting along the track towards them.

Panting as she arrived, she managed to say 'What the fuck was th...' before she saw the tree's face and glowing eyes. Kirsty stood stunned in the moonlight, in awe of the magical creature in front of her. She whimpered, 'What the fuck...'

'*You need a fuckin' thesaurus, hen,*' said the tree.

That made Kirsty and the two lads giggle in sheer disbelief.

'*Hiya Kirsty, Ah'm a wood fairy, nice to meet you. Which one of these two roasters are you shaggin'?*'

Kirsty nodded towards Stevie, who smiled nervously.

'*Oh wow, was it that hummin' Chevignon jumper which first attracted you tae him, hen, or was it the designer blonde hairdo by poodles of Pitlochry?*'

Colin and Kirsty laughed.

'*Whit's wrang wi' Colin here? Still wearing his work overalls, surely that makes the birds as wet as October?*'

Everybody giggled at that one. Kirsty, like Colin and Stevie, seemed to quickly accept the magic tree as fact. She didn't seem freaked out at all.

'Right, ya trio of bawbags, tell me about the problems you're having wi' this Kerr scumbag.'

Chapter Nine

Southern Sun

Over the third and final huge joint, and with Colin pouring more SKOL into the tree's mouth, the three friends told the tree their own tale of woe about the psychotic gangster. The tree listened intently, for once it was the tree who seemed transfixed. When they'd finished telling the tale, the tree gave its verdict.

'So, you two poofters dinnae have the muscle to do this prick in yourselves, and it's doubtful that anyone else fae yer scheme will have the guts to help ye. Ye cannae get rid ae the cunt by grassing on him, either. Hmmmm. that's a tough wan. Normally Ah'd say it's no' ma fuckin' problem, but I like youze. and Ah fuckin' hate bullies.'

'So, you'll help us?' asked Colin.

'Maybe. Ah could get rid of that bully for ye, and there'd be nae comebacks on you. In fact, it would seem like poetic justice if this horrible bullying cunt was vanquished by a wood fairy, eh?'

They all mumbled in agreement. 'So, what's the plan?' asked Stevie.

'Haud yer fuckin' horses, teapots. Before Ah agree to help you, there's two things Ah need fae you.'

The tree then explained to them that the forest ranger had been snooping around the park a bit, pacing out squares around the tree, marking things with spray paint. The tree was worried that he might be felled, to make way for a kids' climbing frame, a water feature, or some other tourist attraction. He wanted them to keep the park ranger away – the guy always came up during the day when the tree was powerless to do anything himself.

Colin said, 'So ye want us to do him in?'

'*Naw, Ah dinnae want yez to dae him in, for fuck's sake,*' snapped the tree. '*I just need him kept away from me until I sort out this wee problem of yours; how you dae that is up to you. Got it? His name is Ronnie Muir.*'

'What's the other thing?' asked Kirsty.

'*Funny it should be you to ask that, hen. As a wood fairy, I draw my powers from my magic sap, problem is, Ah've been stuck here for a fuckin' decade and ma circulation is fucked. It needs to be loosened. Wood fairy legend states that only a fair maiden can smooth the bark on one of my lower branches, and restore aw ma powers tae full strength, it sounds daft Ah ken, but Ah dinnae make the rules.*'

'You want me to massage your branch? What, now?' asked Kirsty.

'*Aye hen, both hands on the right lower branch. It's a tedious necessity, Ah ken, but it'll help us all.*'

'Aye, sure mate, if it helps,' said Kirsty, and she stepped forward and began to squeeze and massage the tree's right hand lower branch.

'*You two, both of ye, skin up on the picnic benches,*' said the tree to the two lads. It had been a long night and Colin and Stevie were happy to do just that a few yards away, while Kirsty did the tree surgeon thing.

Kirsty worked her hands up and down the branch, the tree actually felt warm to her touch. The tree was motionless, but his red glow increased a little as she stroked the branch.

'Well, mate, another crazy night, eh? Are you working the morra?' Asked Colin.

'Aye' said Stevie 'Earlies.' Stevie was by far the fastest roller and was almost finished skinning up. After a minute or so, Colin said, 'Mate, look at this...'

As Kirsty did the sap massage to the tree's branch, the tree glowed far brighter than previously, as Kirsty worked her hands up and down the gnarly wood, the tree seemed to be breathing heavily. Kirsty had also taken off her fleece top and tied it around her waist, now standing there in just her work trousers and a flimsy work blouse, one which barely contained her big, bouncy breasts.

The tree was murmuring now, as his trunk glowed brighter and brighter, illuminating the whole glade against the black sky. 'That's smart as fuck, eh mate?' Said Colin to Stevie, who replied, 'Aye, trippy as fuck, man.'

The tree seemed to be enjoying the magic spectacle, too, its deep voice growing a little breathless as it murmured loudly.

'Aw yes, that's it, restore ma powers, mmmm, change hands hen, that's it, keep goin' harder, faster, aw fuck aye, work that sap, ooooh, that's it, aw fuck, yes hen, ooooooooooooh yes!'

Colin and Stevie stared in disbelief as thick, milky sap exploded from the branch that Kirsty had been massaging, flying in all directions, completely drenching Kirsty. Some splats of it even hit Stevie and Colin too. The tree stood shaking, quivering, eyes closed, then its eyes opened, and there was something new in them – relief, release.

'YA DIRTY CUNT YE, LOOK AT THE STATE OF MA CLOTHES,' said Kirsty, half joking, half seriously pissed off.

'Ooooh, that was brilliant, that shook me right to the roots, you've a magic touch, hen,' said the tree, quickly adding, 'Erm, umm, my sap and powers are renewed, thank you.'

Kirsty simply said, 'Nae bother. Ah'm freezing, Ah'm gawn back to the motor.' As she walked away, she shook her head and repeated to herself, '*Dirty cunt*'.

When Kirsty was out of earshot, Stevie spoke.

'There is nae magic sap, is there? And there's nae wood fairy legend aboot maidens stroking bark, is there, ya filthy fuck?'

'Erm, um, aye there is. Here, geez a draw ae that joint, I love a wee smoke after a good toss ... er, I mean restoration of powers.'

Stevie and Colin looked at each other and laughed aloud.

'*She's a good yin, Stevie, keep a hold of her, if ye can*,' said the tree, in a more matey tone.

'Aye, thanks mate,' said Stevie 'I hope I can. Even if I cannae, at least we'll always be able to rip her aboot that time she was tricked into wanking off a magic tree!'

The tree and the two lads laughed at that, then Colin spoke.

'Just out of curiosity, why do you hate bullies so much, mate? Were you bullied?'

'*Ye dinnae 'hink being forcibly entombed within a fuckin' tree is being bullied, like?*' snapped the tree.

'Awright, awright, nae need to be like that,' said Colin.

'*Ah hate bullies, racists and bigots, always have. Cannae stand the cunts.*'

Stevie said, 'Really? You've said some pretty homophobic stuff tae us.'

'*That's different, that's banter*,' said the tree.

Stevie and Colin looked at each other again.

Stevie continued, 'No' see that as a bit hypocritical, mate? Why do ye hate racism but dabble in homophobic banter?'

'*Well, ye see, that's because I'm black.*'

'Fuck off mate, said Colin, shaking his head in disbelief. 'How are you black?'

'Cos Ah fuckin' am. Ma grandad came over on the *Windrush*.'

'You're talking pish,' said Stevie.

'*How the fuck am Ah no' black? Wait – did you think I was white?*'

'Aye, you've got a Weegie accent, mate', said Colin, adding 'You dinnae sound black.'

The tree's face grew stern at that comment.

'*What the fuck does that mean, ya cunt? Ah dinnae sound black? What the fuck does a black guy sound like? Do ye think there are nae black 'Weegies' as you call them? Ya fuckin' teapots. Ah dinnae sound black? really?*'

The tree then put on a stereotypical deep-south reconstruction post-slavery afro-american voice and did 'jazz hands' with two of his lower branches.

'*Ooh masta, Ah suppose you think I should sounds like this, maybe you should bring me a KFC and a fuckin' watermelon next time, masta, maybe Ah's a gonna sing and dance for ya, masta, ooh lordy well I am just dee wood fairy, I aint no honky, aiiight.*'

'Awright, awright,' said Stevie, 'We get it.'

'*Racist pricks,*' boomed the tree.

'Naw we areny, we're sorry, okay? We just assumed you were white. We're no' bothered what colour you are or were. So, why the homophobia?'

'*Ah've been stuck in here for ten years. There's nae political correctness training in Beecraigs Country Park, dafties. Sorry Ah snapped at ye though.*'

'Ok, mate,' said Colin, tell us how you're gonnae help us wi' our Kerr problem.'

'*Ok. Listen carefully and dae exactly what I tell ye. We'll dae it at the weekend...*'

Chapter Ten

Take Me Away

Colin and Stevie got back to the car to find that Kirsty had already rolled another joint. They smoked it on the drive home, ever paranoid that a police car was about to come round the corner and bust them all. Stevie told Kirsty the tree's plan to get Kerr off all their backs, and that they would need Clare to be there to do it. Kirsty still seemed more wound up by being drenched in naughty tree sap than she was about having just encountered a magic talking tree. Kirsty agreed to the plan, though. The car was soon out of the Bathgate Hills and on the M8. The CD changer in Colin's car had switched to a *Ministry of Sound Clubbers Guide* album, Armand Van Helden's big beat classic track 'You Don't Know Me'.

You don't even know me
You say that I'm not living right
You don't understand me
So why do you judge my life?

Colin bopped his head as he drove, Stevie and Kirsty danced in their seats, the three friends belting out the lyrics – the two lads only knew the chorus, but Kirsty knew the lot. Together, the three of them sounded like a trio of cats being strangled, compared to Duane Harden's vocals, but they didn't care, they were stoned and hyped up. After all, who wouldn't be after such a mental fuckin' Monday?

Colin dropped Stevie and Kirsty off at her place, then drove home to get some shuteye himself. Driving into the little car park beside his home, Colin saw a figure sitting on the low wall which separated the car park from the rows of houses.

It was Clare.

Colin got out of the car, and she ran over to give him a hug. Colin could feel her heart beating through her trendy Ellesse jumper. Clare felt instantly safer in his arms. After assuring Colin that it was safe to go back to her place – as that cunt, Kerr, was out of town for a few days – Colin drove them the short distance there. Upon entering, Clare told him to take a seat while she put the kettle on. Colin was so glad to see her, and not just because he was horny after a heavy weekend – he'd been worried about her. She looked different in jeans, Rockports, and that Ellesse sweater, Colin thought. Younger, somehow, more his own age, without the weekend makeup and killer party dress he usually saw her in. She looked cuter, more attainable, more the girl next door than the model dancing on the podium. Her short, dark hair was tied up, her beautiful eyes even more dazzling than usual.

'Aw naw, am I in love wi' her already?' Thought Colin, as Clare brought through two steaming mugs of tea and sat next to him on the sofa.

Clare didn't say anything about being away at her mum's or about the ongoing Kerr hassle, instead, she produced a pre-rolled joint that they both sat and smoked, whilst slurping down the tea. No sooner had Clare stubbed out the roach than she pounced on Colin, kissing him passionately, sticking her tongue into his mouth. Colin pulled her body tightly against his as they snogged on the sofa. Clare was a slim size 10 but had curves where it mattered, which Colin loved. They were soon disrobing each other eagerly, the only pause to their passion being a momentary giggle as Clare struggled to remove his work overalls that he still had on. That particular *Gordian knot* solved, they headed for the bedroom, Colin excitedly kicking off his steel toe capped safety boots en route. Once there, Clare took Colin in her mouth and teased him until his hips were trembling, stopping at just the right time, as Colin then kissed down her body and returned the favour with his lips and tongue. He soon had her writhing and moaning with pleasure, soaking wet and demanding he be inside her. The two of them made love for almost an hour, reverse cowgirl, doggy, then finishing in missionary, with Bob Marley's Greatest Hits blaring through from the living room hi-fi throughout. As they both collapsed into each other's arms amid mutual post orgasmic glow, Clare spoke.

'Wow, Colin, I think we both needed that, eh?'

'Fuckin' sure,' he said. 'You're pure dynamite.'

Clare was already lighting up a cigarette, quipping 'Aye, yer no' so bad yersel'. FUCK, that's 3am, we're both working the morn, stay if you like, Colin, but we need to actually SLEEP, ken?'

That wasn't a problem to Colin, who nodded and smiled, and within minutes they were both sound asleep in Clare's bed. At some point, as he was nodding off, Colin thought to himself, *'life is good. Weird – but good.'*

Tuesday proved a productive day for Colin and Stevie. Both survived work despite both being a little tired and rough around the edges, after their mental Monday night. Colin took a bit of a ripping at the warehouse for the love-bites that Clare had marked his neck with while in the throes of passion. The usual workforce gags, mostly from the jealous older guys who worked there, for whom sex had been replaced by marriage.

'Do ye no' feed that bird ae yours?'

'Who done that? I bet it was a guy.'

'Are they dug bites?'

The evening saw Colin and Stevie drinking large mugs of tea up in Stevie's bedroom – they'd already shared a joint earlier when en route to the petrol station to get fags.

They'd had a task. The tree had asked them to stop a council employee from going up to Beecraigs, a forest ranger called Ronnie Muir, until after the next weekend. To fix this tricky issue, they had gone to see Wee Kev. Wee Kev was their other friend, who had drifted away from the clubbing scene in the last year or so. Kev had bought a computer and had even had it wired up to that new internet thing, and the main consequence of this was that none of his friends had seen him for months. Kevin was a year older and with his blonde hair in curtains and his thick glasses, he looked like a slightly cooler version of The Milky Bar Kid but would never thank you for pointing that out to him – he'd had enough of that at school.

Kevin had his own one-bedroom council flat and was on the dole, having rattled the speed and the eccies too hard in the first half of 1998, just before he vanished into PC Porn land. He was currently doing a landscape gardening college course up at Oatridge Agricultural College in Uphall, during the day, sent there by the dole on pain of losing his miserable £125 per fortnight Jobseeker's Allowance payment. He'd been pleased to see Colin and Stevie at the door.

Kev's floor was littered with empty beer cans and a few crumpled up tissues, mostly all around the big computer desk. *BOAK.*

There were varying degrees of ashtray spillage dotted around the blue cord-carpeted floor, and the brown sofa was peppered with hot rock burns.

A pizza box sat on the coffee table, and on the wall was a poster of a little green alien with the caption, *TAKE ME TO YOUR DEALER.*

The three friends had caught up over a joint and then gotten down to business. Sure enough, one of the teachers on Kevin's landscaping course happened to be a council forest ranger named Ronnie Muir, who taught the class one day per week – a Thursday. Handily, Kevin thought the guy was an utter prick, so it hadn't taken much cajoling from Stevie and Colin to get him to agree to help them – after all, they were all mates. As they were leaving, Stevie asked Kevin to look up wood fairies on his internet thing. *ASK JEEVES* had produced no conclusive information about wood fairies, so, Colin and Stevie had decided that this new internet thing was shite and would never be that popular – a passing fad.

That morning, As Colin had departed Clare's house to go to work, she had filled him in about the Kerr latest. The police had been dismissive on Monday, saying they couldn't do anything to protect Clare from her ex until he had actually broken a law. Kerr had eventually found Clare's mum's house in East Calder and sat outside it in his car for hours. He hadn't done anything else, but his lurking there had let Clare know that he knew where to find her now. Clare's mum had rung the police again, who actually did move Kerr on when they came, with little trouble – Kerr had sent his message, anyway. He knew where Clare was, though. Now she had nowhere to hide.

Returning to the scheme that very afternoon, Clare had nipped into the pub, where she had quickly overheard someone say that Kerr was 'away on business' – scheme slang for away playing poker with other gangster scumbags in Glasgow, Manchester, or Liverpool. She'd then gone back to her house, eaten, slept, then went up to see if Colin was at home, waiting outside in the summer heat until very late, until he'd eventually returned.

Colin relayed all of this to Stevie as they drank tea in his bedroom, that warm Tuesday night. Their plan that night had been to go see the lassies again.

Dating in pairs is something that's best left to the under 25s – for them, life is usually much simpler. If you're still trying to date in pairs by the time you get to your forties, with all the hang ups and fully developed personality quirks that middle age brings, you're basically fucked – but when you're young, it can be wondrous – 50% less chance of awkward silences.

'So, mate, was she worth the wait?' asked Stevie, referring to Colin's overdue night of passion with Clare.

'A gentleman never tells, man,' replied Colin, giving his mate a knowing wink.

Stevie replied, 'In other words, she was pure dynamite but you're no' gonnae tell me anything specific aboot it until after she's dumped ye?'

'Fuck off, man, this is true love.' Colin smiled as he corrected his mate. Colin then lit up a joint and picked up the PlayStation controller, ready to face Stevie at FIFA. They would eventually head round to Kirsty's to meet up with her and Clare again, that night, and they'd have a blast together, joints, cheap lager, music, banter, and of course, a quick chat about wood fairies and that bastard Kerr. But not until Stevie as Arsenal and Colin as Real Madrid had settled Tuesday night's FIFA grudge match.

Chapter Eleven

Feeling This Way

In a scheme, fuck all ever happens on a Wednesday. It's shite. You see, weekends are mental, Mondays and Tuesdays are for recovering from the weekend, while Thursday is almost the weekend in its own right – it's the trendy pre-club bar, while Friday, Saturday and Sunday are the main event. Wednesday is usually when the weekend party crew finally pluck up the courage to go grocery shopping, visit family or do other sensible, boring shit. Unless you like corrupt top-level European football, Wednesdays are pure pish. Colin and Stevie's mate, Kevin, had college on the Wednesday, though.

Kevin sat and cleaned his glasses at his college desk at Oatridge Agricultural College. His thoughts wandered as his class tutor's voice warbled away in the background as if it were the garbled tedious 'adult' voices in the old Charlie Brown cartoons. WAA WAA WAA.

'Fuckin' hell, man, this is borin' as fuck. I dinnae even want tae be a fuckin' gardener or a landscaper. No sir, I'm going to be one of they dot com millionaires, one day. Who do the dole think they are, sending me here? Like, aye, I've learned a lot, but what gives them the right? Ah thought this new

Labour government and that new parliament we're gettin' in Edinburgh would be aw fir young potential entrepreneurs like me, but naw, it's aw 'get a joab' or 'learn direct' OR we'll stop yer fuckin' giro'. Ah could be at home on the computer wi' a joint, continuin' ma plan for world domination, but aw naw, the man says I've got to be here on this fuckin' course. I dae like the outdoors, and gairdens, but that doesn't mean that's what I want to do for a livin'. Ah like fishin', tae, but that doesn't mean I want to get a job on a fuckin' trawler, oot at sea wi' aw they hurricanes, tidal waves and sea monsters. Christ, I shouldn't have had that joint on the way in today, it's nearly lunchtime and I'm still fuckin' melted from it. Mmm lunch. Bacon 'n' egg doubler from that mocket snack van the day, methinks.

It was guid to see ma mates last night, to catch up and have a smoke, Ah pure love they guys. I feel bad that I dinnae see them at the weekends much now, but I cannae handle any more class As, man. One more eccy or one more gram of speed will put me straight into ward 16, mad house, up at the hospital, for sure. Naw, just weed and the odd beer for me from now on. It was magic to see Stevie and Colin, though. Why the fuck did I agree to help them get rid of that forest ranger cunt, Ronnie Muir? What did they mean? I mean, 'get rid of' is pretty broad. Did they mean in a Goodfellas kind of way? Fuckin' hope no' cos much as I love they two guys and detest the forest ranger, I'm no' daein' a stretch in Saughton for any cunt. Better get ma thinkin' cap on anyway cos he's here to teach us tomorrow. How am I gonnae dae this?

Ah could stick a bomb under his van, but Ah wouldnae ken the first thing aboot bombs.

Ah could poison the cunt, I could Ask Jeeves for a guid poison recipe, no' to kill him, just to make him ill for a week, nah, fuck that, in case he dies by accident.

Ah could tell folk he's touched me up. Hmm, nah, dinnae want anyone to think Ah'm gay.

He's at least a foot taller than me and built like a brick shithouse, so I'll no' be giving him a kickin', besides, that would get me kicked off ma course and the dole would stop ma money. No dole means no giro, nae housing benefit, nae flat and back to live at my ma's – fuck that. Back to smoking oot the bedroom windae and having to have silent danger wanks when I'm not home alone? No way.

Colin and Stevie said they just need this Muir guy to go away for aboot a week, maybe I could get him suspended from his work? Aye, that's what I'll dae. Kev, you're a genius. I'll try to get him suspended tomorrow. That's brilliant, so it is. I knew I'd come up wi' somethin'. Right, so, how am I gonnae dae that? Aye, that might work, that might just work, man...

Chapter Twelve

Pearl River

Thursday afternoon came, and Kevin was stoned again, sitting at the back of his class at Oatridge College. Forest Ranger, Ronnie Muir, whom the students all referred to as 'bawheed', had been teaching the other class at the college that morning, but his afternoon would be taken up by teaching Kevin's class. Muir harboured some contempt for Kevin's class group as he knew they were mostly all reluctant students, sent to the college by edict of the DWP. 'The waster' group, as some of the college staff called them. Muir was about six foot two, a weightlifter, with the physique to match, suntanned from regular holidays to Marbella and with a huge bushy moustache, which made him look like a menacing cross between He-Man and one of the Village People. He knew his shit when it came to forestry and landscape gardening, though. There was a rumour that he used steroids in his bodybuilding, which might have explained his often-short temper.

As Muir started to warble on to the class about the dangers of using ropes to drag lawnmowers up and down steep inclines, Kevin started to zone out, his lunchtime joint having fully kicked in. His gaze drifted from the front of the class to the window, where he could see the college car park. He regarded the forest ranger's white Ford Escort van, which the selfish cunt had abandoned in one of the college's disabled parking spaces. Kevin hated folk who did that. It was a bright, sunny afternoon. Kevin noticed the sun glinting off of an approaching vehicle. As the vehicle entered the car park, he noted that it was a Vauxhall Astra, with police markings. It parked up and two police officers, one male and one female, got out. Both officers noted that a work van was parked in a disabled bay, and Kevin saw the female officer write something in her notebook. After a brief discussion, the two police officers disappeared from view as they entered the main college building.

Kevin, still stoned, turned back to face the class's teacher, trying to look like he'd been paying attention.

'Nice of you to join us, Kevin,' said Muir sarcastically.

Muir didn't get to chide Kevin any further, as with a gentle knock at the door the tweed-suited college principal entered the class and came over to Muir, whispering something in his ear. Muir looked surprised but calmly left the class, heading down the corridor towards reception, barking '5 MINUTES' to the class as he left. The principal was close behind him.

Kevin doodled a smiley face on his notepad and waited.

A few moments later, indistinct raised voices could be heard from down the corridor. One of the voices was Muir's, the other voices were of a male and a female. The voices soon became louder and angrier, a full-scale row had developed in reception. Kevin heard Muir shout, 'Come on then, Ah'll fuckin' show ye,' then the college's main entrance door slammed.

Kevin gazed out of the window to see Muir storming over towards his work's van with the two very disdainful cops following closely behind. Muir stopped at his van's back end to have another rant at the officers, waving his arms in contemptuous fury, as he opened the back of the van and, without looking inside, gestured towards its interior to the police, as if to say 'Voila'. The cops, unimpressed, walked over and had a look into the back of Muir's work's van. Presently, the female officer turned around to face Muir, holding a shoe box. Kevin saw her ask Muir a question and Muir froze for a second, then started waving his arms and ranting again. The summer breeze conveyed Muir's words into the classroom.

'That's no' mine, I've never seen that before. It's no' mine!' ranted the forest ranger. Muir tried to take the shoebox from the female police officer, but she wouldn't let him have it. As they had a little tug of war over the box, the big male copper stepped in to barge Muir out of the way and to try to calm him down. Accidentally, the big cop stood on Muir's toes, who screamed in agony then, as a reflex action, tried to gub the big officer. When things get to that stage with the police, there's only ever one winner. Muir didn't manage to connect his punch to the policeman, but it was a fierce throw, so fierce an air punch that Muir managed to dislocate his own shoulder in the process and lost his footing on the gravel car park surface. He collapsed on the ground, screaming in agony.

The two police officers easily subdued and handcuffed him, then dragged him towards the police car. The last thing Kevin heard was Muir shouting, 'I telt ye, it's no' fuckin' mine. I dinnae ken how that got there.' The entire college watched the incident from their class windows, sniggering, while watching staff didn't know what to say. As the police car left the college car park with an irate Muir handcuffed on the back seat, Kevin let out a satisfied sigh and thought to himself.

'Well lads, job done. You'll no' be hearing from Ronnie Muir the Forest Ranger for a wee while. See, Ah'm a genius.'

Kevin's class was dismissed early that Thursday, so Kev and some of the guys from his course took a long leisurely walk from the college down Ecclesmachan Road, towards Uphall Main Street, from where they could all get busses home. They shared a joint as they swaggered through the countryside back to civilisation. Everybody speculated about why the police had come for Mr Muir, everybody, that is, except Kevin.

Kevin had been a few hours late for college that morning. Nobody had really noticed, Kevin wasn't the type of lad who people noticed much. Just as well, as that morning, nobody noticed him arrive late for college and walk straight over to Ronnie Muir's forest ranger van. Nobody noticed him opening the back of the van and emptying the contents of a large black bin bag into the back. Nobody noticed Kevin casually getting into the driver's side door of the van, the keys of which happened to be left in the ignition. Nobody noticed the van leaving the car park of Oatridge College, driving back down Ecclesmachan Road to Uphall, then turning left to head through Broxburn and along towards Newbridge. However, someone did notice the van doing 80 mph – 30mph over the speed limit – just as it entered Newbridge. Someone noticed that same van again doing 80mph ten minutes later, in exactly the same place and going in the same direction as before. That *someone*, in both of those instances, was a newly installed traffic speed camera. However, nobody noticed the van ten minutes later, as it drove back into the car park at Oatridge College and was parked once more in one of the disabled parking bays, as if it had never been away.

Kevin was a nice lad and a good mate, but he had a dark side, too. When his mates asked him to help them get rid of this Muir cunt for a wee while, he obliged. He had carefully selected what items he was going to plant in the back of the forest ranger's van – enough to get him lifted and into deep shit, both with the polis and with his work, but not enough to pure ruin the cunt's life. The 'present' he left in the van consisted of a shoebox full of pre-wrapped £10 bits of hash, a few wraps of speed which were actually cornflour but were wrapped in pieces of old rave flyposters, for authenticity. He'd also deposited several items of women's lingerie, an old blank-firing athletics starter pistol and a few loose bullets for it, some hardcore porn magazines – some straight, some gay - a small child's denim jacket, a baseball bat, two old Celtic replica jerseys and two copies of the dissident Irish Republican fanzine *An Problacht,* and a jumbo-sized bottle of baby oil. Kev had even taken the time to use his new printer to print off a fictitious drug-dealer 'tick' list.

Quite the sordid, twisted collection of items, carefully curated so as to trigger maximum suspicion, disgust and anger in the average Scottish police officer. Kevin knew his target would get a lot of grief from the polis over this treasure trove, but he also knew that Mr Muir would, eventually, walk away from it, as his fingerprints weren't on any of the items planted in his car. The guy would still be raging, though. Kevin had never been in trouble with the police before, so they'd not get his fingerprints, either. Kev's final *coup de grace* on Muir had been a quick, simple anonymous tip-off call to the police, as a 'concerned citizen'.

Chapter Thirteen

We Are Alive

Upon getting home from work on the Thursday night, Stevie took a phone call from Kev, who filled him in on the progress of 'Operation get rid of Muir'. Stevie had almost pished himself laughing as Kevin matter-of-factly reeled off every item he had planted in the unsuspecting forest ranger's van, and when he almost forgot to mention the speed camera thing, too. Stevie thanked Kev, and told him he owed him one, but Kev was modest about it, all he wanted in return was to be reimbursed for the bits of weed he had sacrificed for this epic prank – and one other small thing. Stevie went round for Colin and the two went out in the car, both of them hee-hawing with laughter at Kevin's audacity. They decided to pay the tree up at Beecraigs a surprise visit that night, to give it the good news about Muir, so, once again, the two mates were driving through the Bathgate Hills in that Peugeot 205.

'Feel The Same' by techno outfit Triple X was blaring from the car stereo. Colin loved the song, Stevie hated it. There weren't many tunes they disagreed over, but this was one.

Stevie said, 'It's pish, man, that's a pure 9pm track. A safe, inoffensive track for when most folk arenae even dancin' yet or are still outside in the queue. Fuckin' elevator music, man.'

We feel the same, this ain't no game
your love is my guiding light
that sees me right
and don't you know
we'll have it all I won't let you fall
your love is my guiding light
that sees me right
and don't you know

Colin replied, 'Nah man, that's pure funky house. Back to basics, four to the fuckin' floor, man, it cannae aw be 'For an Angel', ken? It gets played early in the night to try and get folk unstuck fae the walls and onto the dancefloor, that's surely a good thing?'

'Aye, granted, ye need the lesser tunes to make the bangers sound more epic, eh?'

'If we're aw oot this weekend buzzin' and that comes on, you'll be lovin' it, mate.'

'Aye, yer right. Here, what CD is that?'

'Errr, I think it's *Kiss Anthems*, mate, cheesy but...'

Stevie finished his sentence '... but cheese is often essential to a healthy balanced night, man.'

The two mates laughed as the car pulled into Beecraigs Country Park. It was just before 10pm. They got out of the car and began to trudge over towards the beech tree.

Straight away, they noticed that the tree was already glowing red a little, and it appeared to be singing, and slurring its words.

'"Til nooow, I always got by on my own, Ah never really cared until I met you, and now it chillsh me to the bone, how do Ah get you alo... well well well, looky here, it's the fuckin' Pet Shop Boys, how yez daein'?'

The tree burped, loudly, as Colin and Stevie stood in front of it. Both lads could see a load of empty buckfast bottles and beer cans, and a smashed litre-bottle of Vodka. The tree's facial expression was one of merriment, although it had what looked like severe bruising around one eye.

'*Well, say somethin' lads.*' The tree hiccupped.

Colin asked, 'Eh, are you drunk, mate?'

'*Whit, me? Drunk? Cheeky basturts, but even if Ah wiz, what the fuck's it goat tae dae wi' youze, eh?*'

'You are drunk, mate,' said Stevie, adding 'Hey that's fine wi' us, man.' The tree snapped back at them.

'*Aw, it's fine wi' you, is it? I'm so fuckin' grateful. I have the blessing of the two fuckin' teapots to have a wee swally, well, thank you very much, that's sooooo good of you.*' The sarcasm in the tree's voice was scathing.

'We just came up to see if ye were awright mate, to check if you're still gonnae help us sort oot that Kerr cunt at the weekend, just a social call, really,' said Colin, adding 'So, who got you steamin'?'

'*Had some wee fanny teenagers up here earlier wi' their carry-oot. Wee cunts were drinking here and making some racket; one of the wee bastards was wrecked and smashed a vodka bottle on ma trunk, nearly took ma fuckin' eye oot. Thankfully, it was during daylight hours, so they thought Ah was just a tree, which I suppose I am during the day, to all intents and purposes, eh. But somebody phoned the polis on them, and when the polis came, they ditched aw their drink and did a runner. Aw the vodka from that bottle they smashed plus all the bevvy they hastily poured oot seeped down through the grass intae ma roots and, well, the rest if self-explanatory, is it no'? I am, as you say, pished, drunk, mortal, sozzled, inebriated, intoxicated – fuckin' blootered. Is that a problem?*'

'Naw man,' laughed Stevie and Colin, in unison.

'*But whit if it wiz a problem? Whit the fuck would you two dae aboot it? come ahead, square go, one at a time or both together, Ah'm easy aboot ye baith,*' ranted the tree. Two of its lower branches seemed to curl into fists, making a 'put 'em up' sort of gesture, like Scrappy Doo.

Colin spoke calmly.

'Listen, Sandy, are ye awright?'

The tree stopped ranting; it looked shocked. It let out a sigh, then after a beat, spoke, in a softer, warmer tone.

'*Dae ye ken, it's been a fuckin' decade since anybody has called me by my real name. Wow. Sorry about earlier, lads, Ah'm just drunk, and feeling a bit sad. Ah love you cunts, but.*'

'Is there anything we can do to cheer you up?' asked Colin.

'*Well, actually, if that Kirsty is with you again, my sap needs sortin' oot again.*'

'Naw, no' that, she's no' here anyway,' snapped Stevie.

'*Acht, spoilsports, ok then, skin up, ya bawbags,*' boomed the tree.

Stevie said, 'You've had a lot to drink, mate, are ye sure you can handle a joint right now?'

'*Are you sayin' Ah cannae handle ma weed? It's only your shitey soap bar, for fuck's sake, go on, skin up. I'm a seasoned party animal and drug user.*'

Stevie looked at Colin and shrugged, Colin strode over to the bench and started to build a joint. The tree continued.

'*As to your initial enquiry, aye, I'm lookin' forward to helping you sort out that Kerr bastard, we'll do it on Saturday. Him and his monkey bodyguard, that Fat Carson, they'll no' be bothering you or they birds ever again. Ah fuckin' hate bullies.*'

Stevie replied 'Cool, thanks mate, here, we sorted out your wee Ronnie Muir problem, too, well, at least I hope we did.'

The tree laughed and sniggered, then spoke.

'Ye didnae half. Remind me never, ever to get on the wrong side ae your wee stoner mate, Kevin Mcbride. That was genius.'

Stevie asked, 'How do you ken it was Kevin who did it?'

Colin had just finished rolling the joint and returned, saying, 'Because he's a fuckin' wood fairy, mate, he knows everything.'

All three of them laughed together. Then the tree spoke, excitedly.

'Exactly, Ah'm an all-knowing wood fairy, and don't you fuckin' forget it. It's actually really funny. The polis just aboot had a fit when they saw all that dodgy stuff your mate planked in his work's motor, and because it was a work's motor and Muir denied the stuff was his, the polis had to go and see the council and question his boss and colleagues. The bairn's jacket made the polis think he was a beast, the sexy underwear made his wife think he was cheating on her, the hash was a masterstroke, as was the blank-firing gun, and with the porn that meant he was suspended from his work pending investigation. The Celtic tops, the IRA magazines and the baseball bat were the icing on the cake, cos the arresting officers were both big Rangers fans, let's just say Mr Muir didn't have a very nice time while in custody. The polis got no fingerprints from any of it, though, so he's in the clear. I think he goes back to his work on Tuesday. All he has to worry about now is the two speeding fines from the camera at Newbridge and the fact his missus has chucked him oot. Well done, lads, your mate's a genius, thank you. Mr Muir won't be chopping me doon this week, and by the time he does return here, I'll hopefully be free and long gone, just like we planned. Mr Muir gets his life back, I get my freedom back, you sort out your Kerr problem. Everybody wins. Well, except Mr Muir, but he's a tosser anyway – haw, you, Colin, are you passin' that?'

Colin was trying to smoke and laugh at the same time, not an easy task. He stepped forward to give the joint to the tree, quipping, 'Mate, you've had a skinful, remember, beer and joints together is usually fine, but a joint after a long session of just bevvy, like you've just had, seldom ends well...'

'*Just geez it*,' snapped the tree, so Colin held up the joint to the tree's grinning mouth, braving the alcohol fumes. The tree took two long puffs on the joint, then Colin passed the joint to Stevie.

The tree emitted a low moan, its eyes went all bloodshot, as they usually did after a joint, then the red light glowing within the tree started to flicker and fade.

Stevie was in the middle of complaining that the joint he'd just been passed was almost finished already, when the tree let out a moan and with a 'BLEEEUUURRRGGH' spewed hundreds of gallons of luminous green/yellow vomit all over the surrounding area. Colin and Stevie were pretty much covered from head to toe in tree sick, and just stood there, stunned. Stevie let out a, 'Fuck's sake, man'.

The tree looked seriously ill. All around the base of its trunk was a thick carpet of neon green spew, complete with carrot chunks. The tree's eyes were watering badly.

'Are ye alright, mate?' Asked Stevie.

The tree groaned and moaned, mumbling something about *better out than in*, then it composed itself. In a fragile voice, it spoke.

'*Lads, they Thursday-night doggers will be here soon, so I'd best say au revoir for the evening, sorry, about the whitey, you were right, Ah'm away tae ma fuckin' bed, see ye on Saturday night, ya cunts, dinnae forget, bring them all here, I'll dae the rest, ooooh ma heed.*'

The tree's face vanished from its trunk before Colin and Stevie could say goodbye, so, covered from head to toe in what looked like green ectoplasm from *Ghostbusters*, the two pals trudged back to the car and prepared to drive home – after another joint, of course. Because of the tree vomit they had to strip off their outer clothes and put them in the boot of the car, so as not to spoil Colin's car interior. They were both then sat in their boxers and t-shirts smoking their joint in the car, when four cars full of people arrived and parked up next to them. There were 14 people, four women and about ten guys, the usual dogging ratio, and the doggers wasted no time in gathering around Colin's car, peering in. Some of those peering in were already wanking, mistaking the two pals for fellow dogging enthusiasts.

'Fuck's sake, we better boost now, mate,' said Stevie. 'Dinnae want they doggers to think we're here for that.'

A blast of the car horn and some aggressive gesturing soon cleared the confused doggers out of the way, allowing Colin and Stevie to make good their escape.

'Fuck's sake man, that was a close one. What a riddy,' said Stevie, as they drove back down the Bathgate Hills. On the drive home they smoked their joint and listened to Cypress Hill, rapping along to the music, badly.

Insane in the membrane
Insane in the brain
Insane in the membrane
Insane in the brain

Chapter Fourteen

We Are Alive, Part Two : Disco's Revenge

Friday night found Colin, Stevie, Kirsty, and Clare drinking in their local, *The Castle*. There's nothing like a hot, sunny Friday night in early May, in Scotland, to make people want to gather indoors in a pub with hardly any windows. Colin and Stevie both wore bog-standard central-Scotland weekend male uniform – dark comfort-fit jeans and well-ironed shirts. Colin's dark hair was starting to grow in a bit. Kirsty had her beautiful blonde hair tied back and was wearing a casual green jumpsuit, which made her look a bit like a cross between a superhero and an aerobics instructor. Clare was wearing a long, floaty floral dress, which made her look like a hippy. The pints of lager and the long vodkas flowed; the banter was razor-witted, and someone had put enough money in the pub jukebox to play the whole Oasis album, *The Masterplan*. Good times!

The four friends weren't alone tonight. Joining them around the pool table for a game of Killer were Brian and Lisa, the scheme's cutest couple, both wearing Tommy Hilfiger sweaters. Lisa's best friend Dionne Smart was there too – the quirky, attractive blonde who didn't drink and was married to some boring old twat, though she herself was far from boring. Well-known scheme party animals, Billy and Wee Craig, completed the group of revellers, both of them dressed just like Colin and Stevie – shirt and jeans – Scotland's 90s national dress, to be eclipsed in future decades by the long woolly coat and the grey jogging suit.

Everybody knew each other and got along.

This party of nine had been in the pub since 6pm. What had started as a quiet couple of pints had inevitably morphed into a full-on session.

I'm older than I wish to be
This town holds no more for me
All my life I try to find another way
I don't care for your attitude
You bring me down I think you're rude
All my life I try to make a better day

Dionne, the only sober one, potted the black and thus won the game of killer, by the time the Oasis song 'Rockin' Chair' was blaring in *The Castle*. As the 8-ball sank into the pocket, Dionne blew on the end of her pool cue, like a gunfighter in a movie, and her eight companions clapped and whooped. Auld fellas who had been in the usually quiet scheme pub all day normally left whenever a group of young folk came in to liven the place up, but on this fine May evening, they stayed. *The Castle* was mobbed. People of all ages enjoying their Friday night together in their local pub, amid jukebox music, the clunk of pool balls, laughter, a vast cloud of cigarette smoke and a muted TV in the corner showing Sky Sports News.

Stevie went up to the bar and ordered a round plus nine tequilas. He knew perfectly well that teetotal Dionne wouldn't touch her shot, so Stevie planned to down hers, too. Colin was at the jukebox and put on some dance music – nothing too edgy as it was a pub jukebox, but those

Now that's what I call Music compilation albums usually had four or five bangers on them.

Soon, 'Killin' Time' by techno songstress, Tina Cousins, and then 'Boom Boom Boom' by Dutch eurodance outfit, The Vengaboys, had the whole pub bouncin'. Kirsty took out the two remaining Rainbow Brite eccies and everybody had a wee corner – nine folk sharing two Es might sound a bit like Christ feeding the 5000 with five loaves and two fish, but sometimes the partygoer doesn't want a full E, especially when drinking. Often, for such Friday nights when you have a bigger night planned the following day, a wee half or even just a wee bite will suffice. Pillheads, like most other drug users, can only get so drunk before their brain starts telling them they need something else too, a wee bite was, therefore, just the ticket this Friday night.

The friends gathered around two tables and sat talking about music, films, local gossip, and myriad other topics, as the jukebox continued blaring music, chosen by Colin. Around 30 mins later, as 'Protect Your Mind' by DJ Sakin was playing – the techno version of the *Braveheart* theme – the nine friends all felt the rush together as the first wave of the Rainbow Brites kicked in. Soon they were dancing in the pub, other 'bevvy only' punters looking on in amazement.

When the first E kicks in, the cartoon begins, my friends.

By 10pm, all nine of them had, somehow, in a blur, managed to make their way to, and gain admittance to, Nirvana, the town's only nightclub. It was a nightclub in but two senses; it had a dancefloor, and it was open late. There, its similarity to real proper nightclubs ended. The place was a shithole which they'd all, more than once, vowed never to return to. Yet, here they all were, dancing their arses off to shitey chart-cheese and songs from famous movies which the talentless fuck of a resident DJ genuinely thought he'd be the first DJ to play in a club.

Nightclubs that are the only venue in town are invariably shit, really shit, same faces, same troublemakers, the same music, every fuckin' week. Groundhog Day.

But, sometimes, just sometimes, you can still have a barrie night in one.

Colin, Stevie, Clare, and Kirsty are on the dancefloor cutting some serious shapes to 'Where love lives' by Alison Limerick.

So, why don't you take my hand
Come away, come out of your blues
Boy everything you give, so will I give something to you
I'll take you down, deep down where the love lives
Where love lives, where love lives...

Elsewhere on the dancefloor, a trio of well-turned-out younger women are dancing around their handbags, using pretty bog-standard but acceptable dance moves. Most eyes in the dreadful venue are on them, not for their choreography but for the shortness of their skirts and sharpness of their dress. Next to them, some wasted dude in a checked Burberry shirt is doing robotic dancing, and failing miserably at it, yet seems to be enjoying himself. Beside him, his mate, a lanky geezer wearing a blue Sonetti tee-shirt and black jeans, with black Rockports, is doing the running man dance. Alas, it appears to be the only dance move he knows, and to make matters worse he's wearing white sports socks with his black shoes and black jeans – he looks ridiculous with every step amid the disco lights. White socks with dark shoes = social suicide.

Nearby, dance two couples in their early 30s, clearly of the 'one drink too many after work' ilk, whose 'zany to them but would be pish boring to us' night is nearing its end, rather than just beginning, as with most of the other patrons. The two fellas are suited and booted, the two ladies appear to still be in office wear, too. They dance like all white middle-class 30-somethings do – terribly. Think Eddie Murphy's 'white man dance' comedy bit, but with even less grace. The two guys keep looking around from time to time, clearly trying to ensure that no other men are ogling or trying to dance with 'their' women, like two primeval ape creatures guarding their territory, yet all four in that party seem to be enjoying themselves. Being a shite dancer is actually fine, it's better than being a killjoy cunt who doesn't dance at all.

Two chubby lassies in their 40s are also giving it big licks on the dancefloor, both holding bottles of Bacardi Breezer. There's even an old geezer in his 50s who looks utterly pished, trying to do a solo John Travolta impression on the dancefloor, swinging his lit cigarette about as if it were a raver's lightstick, completely oblivious to what a tit he looks.

The mediocre resident DJ is now playing a dance remix version of 'Stuck in the Middle With You' by Stealer's Wheel. More drunken or eccied bodies flock to the dancefloor with a collective 'waaaaay' as the opening lyrics kick in.

Well, I don't know why I came here tonight
I've got the feeling that something ain't right
I'm so scared in case I fall off my chair
And I'm wondering how I'll get down the stairs...

The talentless DJ thinks he's Paul fuckin' Oakenfold for dropping this track, which he really isn't. The movie, *Reservoir Dogs,* was nearly six years ago. Nevertheless, the eclectic mix of people on the dancefloor – and, those hanging around its fringes swigging drinks, smoking fags or eyeing up the talent – are seriously digging the vibes. Some on the dancefloor clap along, a few guys are even modifying their dance steps to mimic Michael

Madsen's weird dance from the film, at the bit where he cuts off that cop's ear.

Superbore DJ then tries to take it to the next level and drops 'The Good Life' by the New Power Generation, next. The Dancing Divas remix, obviously. In the late 90s, it's that song everybody loves but nobody knows what it's called, or who sings it, mostly due to the fact the original version, released in 1997, was dreadful and only made the top 30 of the charts, with this gem of a remix by Dancing Divas hiding as the 4th track on a limited edition maxi EP release. In truth, before the internet was a thing, virtually no cunt knew who Dancing Divas were, either. Nonetheless, DJs know all about this hypnotic, catchy euphoric track and it's played everywhere.

As the opening bass kicked in, the whole dancefloor crew let out a little 'OOWA OOWA' – those around the dancefloor were also starting to sway and dance a little bit more, as the seven-minute track meandered towards its mind-blowing drop. Every 90s clubber knows this tune, even if they still don't know what it is or who sang it.

The good life, one day that's what I'll be livin'
Fantasy never hurt nobody, whatever chills the illin'
When the everyday gets on your last one
Give it up and go
To the place in everyone's future
The good life, one day we'll
Good life, one day that's what I'll be livin'
Fantasy never hurt nobody, whatever chills the illin'
When the every day gets on your last one
Give it up and go
To the place in everyone's future
The good life, one day we'll know.

Against all odds, this turgid, boring glorified disco bar was now actually jumpin'. There were hands in the air, dancefloor hugs, even people dancing on tables. Even the ogre-esque bad-tempered, corrupt bouncers, lurking on the fringes, seemed to be relishing the atmosphere. Some of the better looking, fitter bar staff were even up dancing on the bar. You see, no matter how shite the venue, all working class people need to have an amazing time is good music, good 'stimulation' and a dancefloor – it doesn't matter if the venue is the Arches, Cream, Ministry of Sound, or some small-town dive – if the basic ingredients are there, there's usually an epic time.

Colin and Stevie are dancing side by side, doing their own, more accomplished, version of the running man dance, making the white socks with dark shoes guy look even more of a tit, but nobody cares. Kirsty and Clare are dancing together, up close and personal, practically lap-dancing for each other. Neither of them is even remotely bi, but they're friends, they're having a great time on a Friday night, they're wasted, and they know that their outlandish faux lesbianism in time to the music is drawing the gaze of almost everybody in the disco.

The DJ moves seamlessly into two tracks by Livin' Joy – 'Don't Stop Movin'' and the much better 'Dreamer'. Kirsty and Clare uncouple from each other to, once again, dance beside Colin and Stevie. All four of them are happy, buzzin', and sweating. Nearby are their companions this evening. Brian and Lisa are merrily snogging up against a pillar, as usual. Craig and Billy are cutting shapes near the bottom of one of the staircases that leads onto the dancefloor, but by far the most impressive sight among them is wee Dionne, the one who never drinks. In her silver halter-neck minidress and with her shoulder-length, platinum blonde hair, all eyes were on her. Nobody danced as well as Dionne, nobody looked as good dancing as Dionne, nobody's general appearance or manner in a club more typified the late 90s clubber, than that of Dionne. People weren't perving at her, they were in awe of her. Every dancefloor needs a few Dionnes, be they male or female.

Here we lie all alone, am I dreaming?
Your heart's smooth, my soul is unbelieving
Now you see the me and I'm feelin', I'm feelin'
I feel your hands, your lips, the heat of your body
Whisper you love me, say you love me
Please, just love me down and never leave me
I'm a dreamer

Livin' Joy moved into DJ Quicksilver's epic track 'Belissima' and the party in the local disco-bar carried on. Colin, Stevie, and their pals were having a great night, and on only a few drinks and a wee nibble of an E each. The atmosphere was good; the crowd, on the same wavelength; the music was a bit cheesy but still good. But, of course, all good things must come to an end.

The DJ was under strict instructions from the management to keep the music styles he played varied. As the crowd expected the next banging dance track, instead they got deafened by the unmistakable *DINGALINGALING* that heralds the start of ... 'Baggy Trousers' by Madness. The atmosphere in the disco changed.

Colin, Stevie, Kirsty and Clare treated the *DINGALINGALING* as a klaxon warning them to leave the dancefloor immediately, though as they climbed the steps away from it and headed to the bar, they still all did the trademark 'knees up' walk-dance that most people associate with this song and with the band Madness itself. They reached the bar and Clare ordered four bottles of water. £8. Eight fuckin' quid – almost as dear as a 'proper' drink. Still, they all needed the hydration.

Colin stood behind Clare and wrapped his arms around her waist, resting his chin on her shoulder. Stevie and Kirsty were having a long overdue snog, after all that dancing. They'd all passed the peak of their E dunt now and thoughts naturally turned to quieter, more relaxed surroundings. As they walked over to lean on the barrier railing to look down upon the dancefloor, they were greeted with what one can only describe as clubber's hell – a 1999 version of Dante's Inferno.

The dancefloor was still bouncing, but very differently – it was carnage.

Oh, what fun we had
But did it really turn out bad
All I learnt at school
Was how to bend, not break the rules
Oh, what fun we had
But at the time it seemed so bad
Trying different ways
To make a difference to

The hexagonal dancefloor was now a mass of jumping bodies, instantly more like a heavy metal mosh pit. Madness being played in discos often ends badly.

'Here, where did aw they guys come fae?' Stevie asked his friends. 'Fuck knows', all three of them replied in unison, each with a shrug of the shoulders.

Stevie was referring to around 12 huge skinhead guys who, it seemed, had appeared from nowhere. They were right down at the front of the dancefloor just beside the DJ booth and doing the old punk 'pogo' dance, giving it fuckin' laldy, actually. They were only skinheads in the hairless sense – all were dressed smart casual, like a wee mob of Grant Mitchells.

The sudden switch by the DJ from commercial dance to Madness had caught the dancefloor off guard. The three beautiful lassies who had been handbag dancing, whom most men in the place had been watching lecherously on the dancefloor, managed to avoid the coming storm, too, having slipped quietly up some steps and back to their table safely. Many of the rest of the revellers weren't so fortunate. Dancing to Madness invariably involves either doing the band's trademark zany funny walk, or jumping around like a lunatic, raising one's knees and swinging one's elbows about. When jumping, it's actually natural to raise your elbows, to protect yourself. But scores of drunk or melted people all doing that while packed together on a relatively small dancefloor, under disco lighting, whilst trying to hold drinks in their hands, well, it just doesn't work. The scene Colin, Stevie, Kirsty, and Clare saw was more akin to the huge brawl scene at the end of the movie *Blazing Saddles*, than it was to *Human Traffic*.

Burberry check shirt guy and his 'white socks with black shoes' mate were in among some of the pogoing skinheads, doing their best to join in with their crazy dance. But then, Burberry shirt guy took an accidental but hardly surprising elbow to the face and staggered back, blood pishing from his nose. White socks guy saw it and went over to try to remonstrate with the skinhead who'd done it. The skinhead turned around, gave a gesture as if to say, 'I can't hear you', and turned around to start bouncing with his mates again. When 'white socks', with more force, grabbed his shoulder from behind to try to gain his attention again, the skinhead turned and gubbed him a beauty, sending him flying back across the dancefloor and straight into the two fat birds, who, with the force, fell backwards against the side of the dancefloor, smacking into the wall and ending up on the deck, soaked from head to toe by the contents of their spilled Bacardi Breezers. White Socks guy came crashing down on top of them, having slipped on drink spilled on the floor during the ongoing Madness melee. His own near-full bottle of Newcastle Brown Ale had landed on the floor, too, showering the two lassies on the deck with thick beer foam, adding to their misery.

The older geezer, who was still using a lit cigarette as a glowstick, came over to try to help the three figures on the ground, probably in the hope that at least one of the lassies would shag him for his gallantry, but he was barged off balance by more pogoing dancers, slipped on the same puddle of spilled drink and was sent sprawling into the heap of people up beside the wall. His cigarette bounced off the wall as he fell, and showered them all with sparks and ash, before it fell, still alight, down the low-cut top that one of the lassies on the ground was wearing. She, in turn, shrieked in pain and anger as she rose from the ground, lifting up her top in order to get rid of the lit cigarette now wedged between her large, overly pendulous breasts. A young lad dancing nearby instinctively noticed that there was exposed tit about and stared briefly, enraging the poor lassie even more, to the point that she kicked him hard in the balls, but she then slipped backwards while doing so, back onto the ground among the spilled drinks and fag ash. The other three fallers were back on their feet. White socks guy, the other chubby lassie and the old geezer were all utterly drenched in drink, absolutely dripping from head to toe. They all helped the other lassie to rise again. The lass who had just got up was in an enraged stupor, with some justification. The spilled drink on her dress made it look like she had just pissed herself. Her pal wasn't looking much better. Both's hair, makeup and clothes were utterly ruined – drenched in drink and covered in black marks from the wall and floor. In their rage, they both set about beating up white socks guy on the dancefloor, who had no option but to protect himself with his arms. The old geezer tried to play peacemaker by pleading with the lassies to calm down, but, well, no human being in history has ever calmed down after being told to 'calm down'. One of the lassies hooked the old geezer on the chin by accident as he tried to stop the fight, and once again he found himself on the deck, rolling in liquid fag ash filth, as the two lassies got white socks guy down onto the deck and started to boot him with their high heels. Burberry shirt guy had just returned from the toilets, where he had gone to remedy his bloody nose. Still holding a big ball of toilet paper around his swollen, bloody beak, he tried to pull the two lassies off white socks guy, but the bouncers finally arrived and all they saw was a guy in a Burberry shirt trying to manhandle two lassies. He was soon dragged off the dancefloor by three gorillas wearing *Steadyrock* bouncer jackets and Doc Martens, and, for him, Friday night was over. His ejection from the premises at least meant that the bouncers saw white socks guy on the deck and were able to rescue him from the two chubbers' vicious assault, though, being bouncers, they immediately chucked white socks out, too. He was carried out by four bouncers, one on each limb, screaming that he had done no wrong.

There were half a dozen similar, even worse, incidents involving other clubbers that happened on that same dancefloor at the same time.

It hadn't helped that the disco's DJ had fucked off to the toilet after putting on *Baggy Trousers* AND queuing *One Step Beyond* by the same band to come on next. The dancefloor, a sea of barging elbows and flying limbs, had claimed a dozen or more victims in the time it had taken those two Madness songs to play. All around the dancefloor, women cried, men dusted themselves down or nursed burst faces, further fights seemed imminent. The four office workers thought they'd managed to escape the carnage, but as they reached the club foyer and the two office lassies used the payphone to call for a taxi, their two drunk male companions tried to complain to bouncers and staff about the near riot that they had just escaped. The bouncers, being bouncers, weren't prepared to listen to any shite from these middle-class twonks, and politely told them, 'get tae fuck, yer barred'. The two suited and booted idiots didn't listen and upped the ante with their weedy remonstrations and were both promptly grabbed from behind and speedily marched towards the fire escape, which was ajar because of the summer heat. Here, in the one part of this shitey disco-club that wasn't covered by CCTV, these two idiots learned the meaning of the word 'pain', with the door trolls taking care not to leave any visible marks on them, so that their injuries could be ascribed to 'resisting ejection'. They did nothing to either start or worsen the melee on the dancefloor, but the two twonks paid the price on behalf of everyone that did. It wasn't fair, but, fuck, life's no' fair, is it? For a final *coup de grace,* the door trolls told the two female office lassies that they had seen their dates talking to two young women back inside the club, so, the women took the taxi to themselves, away up the road thinking they'd been ditched, while the two twonks were condemned to a weekend of aching ribs and wanking.

Stevie and Colin's other pals all avoided the carnage, too. Brian and Lisa had followed their usual M.O. and had fucked off in a taxi without telling anyone. Nobody minded that, they were such a nice couple. Billy and Wee Craig had danced to Madness for a bit, then sensibly retreated to the bar at the other side of the club, to do tequilas and to look for some women to spraff to. As for Wee Dionne, some guy had grabbed her arse from behind on the dancefloor just before Madness came on and she had reacted by spinning around and throwing her pint of iced water all over him, utterly drenching him. She had then vacated the dancefloor and calmly went to sit with some people she knew from work, without even looking back at the guy she had just soaked – that was Dionne, coolness personified.

Colin, Stevie, Kirsty, and Clare had watched the mayhem on the dancefloor for a good ten minutes, giggling and shaking their heads as they drained their bottles of water. It had been a good night, but this was a movie they had all seen at this shitey venue far too many times before. They all agreed that it was time to go up the road. They paired off and headed for their respective toilets, before leaving, as the strains of '*You're Gorgeous*' by Babybird filled the smoky air of the disco. An apt song, when half of the punters were by now either drenched in bevvy or blood, covered in floor or wall slime, stinking of fag smoke and either pished or eccied. So goes the world, in those one-club towns. Nobody minds the irony.

Chapter Fifteen

Bla Bla Bla

Stevie and Colin were standing at the long urinal in the men's bogs, at its far end, just where the four cubicle stalls began.

'Fuck's sake, Stevie, ma bellend is a like a fuckin' acorn, see they fuckin' Rainbow Brites, man...' said Colin, still sounding eccied and loved up.

'Mine tae, mate, dinnae worry, it'll be awright after a joint and some TLC fae Clare,' said Stevie.

E and speed can often make some guys' penises temporarily shrivel up a bit. It's because of dehydration, but this can usually be overcome by a relaxed environment and the right touch from a lover – and when it does finally get going, it's like a fuckin' iron bar.

They both laughed, then continued chatting, as they zipped up and turned to the sinks on the other wall, opposite the cubicles, to wash their hands.

'Clare was saying that she's had to get tablets fae the doctor because of this business wi' Kerr, man, we really need to sort this oot tomorrow night, mate, Kerr has to go. Do ye really think our man up at Beecraigs will sort him oot? What was the plan again, anyway? Ah'm melted, man,' said Colin.

'We get Kerr on his own up to Beecraigs and our big pal will do the rest, one way or another, this shite ends tomorrow night, mate. We stitched up that forest ranger cunt Muir for him, so he'll help us,' said Stevie.

The two friends turned and exited the toilets, meeting up with Kirsty and Clare in the club Foyer, where they waited in the queue to use the club's only payphone, in order to get a taxi. Kirsty had clearly been talking to Clare in the toilets.

'A magic fuckin' tree? Aye, right then. That's yer fuckin' plan? That's our fuckin' grand strategy? A fuckin' tree? Really? Are youze on the LSD or whit?' Clare asked.

Colin was quick to speak. 'Sssshhhh, Clare, no' here. Look, it's a nice night, let's walk up to your bit, Kirsty, it only takes about 15 minutes, we can tell Clare the whole story on the way home. Fuck the taxi, let's go.'

The four of them thus enjoyed a lovely summer night stroll home, melted, talking absolute nonsense, and doing their best to give Clare a clear explanation of the whole wood fairy thing. She took some convincing, but by the time they were back at Kirsty's and smoking a few joints while listening to Massive Attack, she was fully on board, after all, it's not that far-fetched, is it? Getting an enchanted ex-raver trapped inside a tree to help you run your worst enemy out of town, is it?

As Colin and Stevie had left the toilets, they had no idea that their every word had been heard by two people, neither of whom knew each other. In the cubicle nearest the urinals, a gigantic bearish oaf of a man was struggling to squeeze out a big shite, having overindulged in fried pizza and copious amounts of lager all day. That man was William Carson Forbes, from the scheme, and Fat Carson had heard every word of the vague threats aimed at his boss and 'mate', Gavin Kerr. Carson had waited until he was sure that they two wee pricks from the scheme had left, then, after wiping his gigantic arse and not washing his hands, headed from the toilets to the payphone in the Foyer, to phone Kerr and alert him to what he'd heard.

Unbeknownst to both Fat Carson and to Colin and Stevie, the second cubicle's occupant had also taken a keen interest in *eariwigging* on their conversation re. Kerr, but for another reason. This was another tall man, but stronger, fitter, and older, nursing a bloody nose and some bruises. With his muscular physique and bushy moustache, he looked like a cross between He-Man and one of the Village People. This guy had endured a dreadful week thus far, wrongly arrested and beaten up by the police, then accused of drug dealing, paedophilia, child abduction, being a pervert, firearms offences, materially supporting a proscribed terrorist organisation and, in the police's eyes, the only crime worse than any of those – being a Fenian. Not only that, but he had been suspended from his job and thrown out by his wife, despite his innocence and no charges being brought against him. Then, to top it all off, he had went out for a pint tonight to try to forget it all, had ended up in the local shithole disco, been knocked back by every lass he spoke to and had been elbowed full force in the face while trying to dance to his beloved *Madness*. Yet now, by chance of overhearing a conversation in the dreadful disco bogs, he knew exactly where and when his tormentors would be, tomorrow night. For Ronnie Muir the suspended forest ranger, there was now a chance for some payback...

Chapter Sixteen

Nothing But You

The small gathering back at Kirsty's didn't last long but was enjoyed by all. After a few joints, some chat and many cups of tea, the two fledgling couples both decided they had other needs to see to – it was still the weekend, after all.

Colin and Clare left to go back to Clare's place, both in the grip of the raging eccy-horn. Some people get horny *on* Ecstasy, others get hornier on the comedown. Colin and Clare were just plain horny. Colin drove as Clare reached across to rub and squeeze his dick through his jeans, at one point almost causing them to veer off the road, but they made it to her place safely.

As soon as Clare's front door shut behind them, the two were kissing passionately up against it, Clare lifting her floaty floral dress over her head to reveal her beautiful, smooth, statuesque body in red bra and thong, while Colin unbuttoned and removed his casual shirt to reveal his milky white, wiry torso, tossing the garment aside. He reached behind Clare's thighs as she instinctively jumped up to wrap her legs around his waist, and the two carried on kissing while Colin carried her through to her bedroom in that position, before laying her down on the bed. Colin slipped out of his jeans and boxers but before he could join the giggling Clare on her bed, she looked up at him and held out her hand like a *STOP* sign.

Clare then shuffled to the edge of the bed, looked up at Colin, winked at him, then proceeded to give him the best blowjob of his entire life. Some women *think* they give good blowjobs but actually don't do much other than blandly mimic vaginal sex with their mouths – but not Clare. Colin stood there and felt her engulf his bellend with her wet lips, her swirling tongue, her spit, and her hot breath. Clare even moaned sexily whilst doing it, as she enjoyed giving head. This had the normally calm and collected Colin gasping and groaning, as she pleasured him. Colin could also see that Clare was touching herself with her hand at the same time, too, and this made him throb harder and gasp louder. For a brief moment in his ecstatic delirium, he noted to himself something in his head.

'Nae wonder that bastard Kerr is pissed off that he's no' gettin' this anymore', but the inappropriate thought came and went.

Clare was now stroking and squeezing his balls as she took almost his entire length down her throat and Colin was howling in pleasure, he looked down at Clare pleasuring him, now completely naked, she was so beautiful, and he was just lovin' this bliss. Then, Colin felt a tickling sensation begin to grow in his groin and genital area. His balls were tightening, too, he felt a slight anxiety that he was going to explode too soon...

'Mmmm, did ye like that? My turn now, lover,' said Clare, smiling, still cradling Colin's dick, dribbling wet from her mouth attention, in her hands and smiling up at him. She'd sensed his 'tickly bit' so had stopped the blowjob.

Colin had hissed slightly as Clare had removed her lips from him, but he instinctively knew why she had, and he was glad she'd stopped. He needed to be inside her, he needed to feel her insides clench, he needed to fuck her – and that's exactly what she wanted.

'Lie back, darlin', said Colin, and she did. The two kissed again, and Colin worked his mouth down her body, paying particular attention to her stiff nipples, before burying his face in her sweet wetness. Clare moaned as Colin's lips and tongue worked on her clitoris and teased her labia gently, and with plenty of wetness, from her and from him. Clare loved this and came hard after a while, her hips bucking like she was riding in a rodeo, almost breaking Colin's neck as she cried out in pleasure. Clare then got on top of Colin and rode him in cowgirl and then in reverse cowgirl, really using all of her strength to enjoy him for as long as possible, all the while Colin's hands were all over her body as he pushed upwards into her, matching her every delicious stroke. Clare was in a sexual frenzy and came again whilst riding him, Colin loving the feel of her wetness dripping down onto his balls as she swore and groaned, owning him, using her body to let him know that he was her plaything, now, and that he was her chosen man. Both of them were caked in sweat and full of bliss as a breathless Clare slipped off him and bent over on all fours on the bed, facing away from him, wiggling her small, firm ass, and saying teasingly 'C'mon Colin, dinnae stop'. In a flash, Colin was easing himself into her from behind, both of them gasping as he started to fuck her again. Their sexual ecstasy, the real actual ecstasy, the weed, and the pure buzz of being together had them moving together in the doggy position for what seemed like a beautiful eternity; the outside world mattered not, only they did, together – they were an island of pure bliss. As Clare came, loudly, for a third time, shrieking in pure delight, it was all too much for Colin, who grabbed her hips and pulled her right down onto his length, so deep that his taut balls were touching her skin, as he cried out in joy, reaching orgasm deep inside Clare, filling her with what seemed like a Danube of cum. He stayed inside her for a few minutes, still enjoying the feel of her, and her of him. Sex with a condom is, at best, really good. Sex without one, good sex, mind, touches your fuckin' soul. And these two accidental star-crossed lovers were no different. They snuggled up together for a while to recover, all smiles, strokes, and gentle affirming kisses. The lovers' *La Petite Mort* of post-coital bliss was short lived at first, as Clare told Colin to go and build a joint, and then, because he was already out of bed, to also make them a cup of tea, too, which he happily did – it was when he agreed to do both of those things while Clare just lay in bed doing fuck all that he realised – he was definitely in love with her now. Soon he returned to bed with two steaming mugs of tea and a nice fat joint of soap bar, and their *La Petite Mort* resumed once more, a beautiful, intimate, post-orgasmic, eccy sleep, wrapped around each other. It was about 4am, so the summer dawn was already creeping over the 1999 sky.

After Colin and Clare had left her place, Kirsty had told Stevie to build a joint and to make some more tea and put some decent, chilled tunes on, which he did. They were both really horny, absolutely gagging for it, yet were also both a bit rough from the Rainbow Brites and the drink – they needed another joint. Kirsty left Stevie on the sofa skinning up as she went through to the bedroom. Once there, she got changed out of her smart and sexy green jumpsuit – it didn't exactly lend itself to easy removal. Instead, she slipped into a gorgeous little *Janet Reger* lacy negligee, then covered it with a short blue satin bathrobe that she'd acquired on a hen-do a few months earlier. She untied her blonde hair and let it fall down to her shoulders, before spraying herself with her expensive, fashionable Paco Rabane perfume and a tad of *Impulse* body spray. She then turned to gaze into her full-length mirror. She looked fucking hot, and she knew it. For a brief moment, she wondered what it would be like to snog herself passionately. Would she like it? What would it be like? Did thinking that make her bi? She had nothing against being bi but was pretty sure that she wasn't. No, in her eccied and slightly drunk but fully aware current state, she wanted cock – Stevie's cock, to be precise – she'd been looking forward to it all evening. Satisfied that her big tits looked amazing in her negligee, Kirsty headed back through to the lounge.

On the wall was the movie poster for *Pulp Fiction*. The curtains were drawn, and the only light in the room came from the muted TV – stuck on MTV Dance – and the small corner lamp beside the sofa, where Stevie sat puffing on a joint that he had just sparked up. Stevie had chosen well when asked for chill tunes – Pink Floyd's 'The Division Bell' was playing. As the epic guitars and pained vocals of *What do you want from me?* filled the room, Kirsty glided across the grey carpet towards the sofa and Stevie. Stevie's eyes were out on stalks watching her, Kirsty's quick-change act had taken him by surprise, the good way.

As you look around this room tonight
Settle in your seat and dim the lights
Do you want my blood, do you want my tears?
What do you want?
What do you want from me?

By the time she stood right in front of him and slipped off the blue bathrobe to reveal her tremendous body wrapped tantalisingly in her negligee, Stevie was harder than iron, laughing briefly inside his head at his earlier anxiety about the E-induced acorn-dick. Kirsty felt so aroused from the obvious effect that she was having on him that she felt some of her own wetness drip down her inner thigh.

Unlike Clare and Colin, these two didn't even make it through to the bedroom. They spent the next hour or so fucking deliciously on the soft grey carpet of the lounge, every position they could think of, plus a few that they discovered by accident. Their erotic antics gained them both many carpet burns that night, but they didn't give a flying fuck. By the time the beautiful, atmospheric song *High Hopes* was playing on the big high-stacked stereo hi-fi, Stevie and Kirsty were enjoying epic simultaneous orgasms together in the missionary position.

The grass was greener
The light was brighter
With friends surrounded
The nights of wonder

It was there, on the now damp carpet, that they both eventually passed out, after their passionate exploits, and after finishing the joint and downing some cold tap water, of course. They too, drifted off blissfully wrapped around each other, while having a playful argument about the album they'd just fucked to, *The Division Bell*. Kirsty didn't mind it, but decried it as being 'Floyd Light' as Roger Waters was no longer in the band when it was recorded, and without Roger Waters, there could be no true Pink Floyd. Stevie had countered that there had been several 'Floyd albums since Waters had left the band in a huff, and that he preferred the later stuff as it was more uplifting, more their generation. It wasn't much of an argument, really – they were both too loved up. Eventually, they would wake in the early morning, and head through to Kirsty's bed for some actual sleep. After all, it was Saturday now. And we all know what was planned for Saturday…

Chapter Seventeen

For An Angel

By the Saturday afternoon, all four of them were sitting in Wee Kevin's living room, smoking joints, drinking cups of tea, and finalising their strategy, while Mike Oldfield's 'Tubular Bells 3' was playing, in a tinny sound emanating from Kev's PC speakers. They'd convened at Kev's place because they needed some weed and Kevin always had plenty. They also wanted to pick Kevin's brain and ask his advice, for all were at a loss about how best to lure Kerr up to Beecraigs – Kevin was good at thinking up that kind of stuff, as his shockingly effective number on that forest ranger erse had shown. The other reason they'd assembled at Kev's was more practical – they couldn't risk being spotted out and about in the scheme in case Kerr or his minions caught up with them there, far away from the shield of their magic wood fairy protector. After all, this was the weekend Kerr had set as the deadline for Clare to repay the cash she 'owed' him, and Kerr never missed a chance to collect a debt.

Kevin's living room was mingin'. The coffee table was littered with skinning up stuff, food cartons, old newspapers, dirty mugs, and loose change – coppers, mostly. The carpet hadn't been hoovered for a while and there was a sort of dank, musty male smell lingering in the air – a mixture of weed, sweat, farts and stale cum. On the floor, poking out from under one of the armchairs, was a copy of the porno magazine, 'Razzle'. The

Mike Oldfield track *'Man in the rain'* played in the background – it was a very deliberate rehash of his old song *'Moonlight Shadow'* but with Pepsi Demaque, of *Pepsi and Shirley* fame, replacing Maggie Reilly on vocals. Rehash or not, it was still a barrie song.

> *You can't stay, no, you can't stay.*
> *You're no loser, there's still time to ride that train*
> *And you must be on your way tonight.*
> *Think anew right through, you're a man in the rain.*
> *How's it feel when there's time to remember?*
> *Branches bare, like the trees in November.*
> *Had it all, threw it all away.*
> *Now's the time to walk away.*

Several strategies were mooted for luring Kerr up to Beecraigs on his own. The most obvious one involved Clare pretending that she wanted to get back with him, then suggesting they go for a drive up there, but that wouldn't work, firstly because Kerr would see Colin's car parked up as he drove into Beecraigs with Clare and would know something was up, secondly, though he was a bonehead, Kerr wasn't fucking stupid.

As the five friends debated what to do, Stevie got up and paced around the room as that usually helped him to think. As he paced by Kevin's computer – the screen of which was asleep in standby mode, he hit the spacebar on the keyboard and the monitor sprung to life, the chug-chug whir of the PC drive starting up. The screen was instantly filled by an enlarged thumbnail of a porn image of a dead-eyed young woman in an Ann Summers sailor-girl outfit, using an old-fashioned naval telescope to masturbate– Kevin had, it seemed, had some action last night, too.

'Fuck's sake, man,' exclaimed Kev, leaping from his armchair and lurching towards the computer desk in order to close that embarrassing window, as Clare, Kirsty, and Colin all laughed their heads off. Stevie wasn't laughing, though, he was thinking. He asked Kevin to look up Beecraigs Country Park on the internet thingy. Kevin found a page all about it on Microsoft's *Encarta* encyclopaedia. There was a wee bit about the Cairnpapple iron-age site, and a few sentences about how that part of the Bathgate Hills had virtually no light pollution and was popular with stargazers.

Stevie blurted out. 'Ya fucker, that's it, we tell everybody we're going up to Beecraigs tonight at dusk to go stargazing when we're melted. We make sure Kerr knows that we'll be up there, just us, trying to have a quiet night. Kerr thinks me and Colin are hippie pussies so that'll play right with him, he knows he can take us without backup, so he'll come. He will.'

Everybody else seemed a bit sceptical, but in absence of a better idea, they agreed on that course of action. The next few hours were spent phoning up certain people from the scheme to ask what they were doing tonight, people whom they knew would blab. Stevie and Colin went to *The Castle* for an afternoon pint during the football, when the pub was rammed, making sure that they told all and sundry that they were going stoned stargazing that night. Wee Kevin went to the bookies and did the same thing, while Clare and Kirsty stayed in Kev's and phoned up minor drug dealers, claiming to be looking for weed, but asking for grass, as they knew local dealers had none, but knowing that their reason for wanting the weed would get back to Kerr via the scheme grapevine. Most of the scheme dealers were so loyal to Kerr that it was inevitable that he'd find out where his prey would be and at what time – for once, it was hoped, the paranoid nutter Kerr's local espionage system might just work against him.

Chapter Eighteen

Synths and Strings

Saturday the 8th of May 1999. Scotland's parliament had just reconvened in Edinburgh after a near-300-year hiatus. An Irish TV comedy called *Father Ted* had just won all the comedy awards at the BAFTAS. The long-awaited new *Star Wars* movie had just come out. British and American forces were bombing the fuck out of fascist Serbia's army of genocidal maniacs in Kosovo. Hibernian FC had just been promoted back to Scotland's top flight, after a season in the lower tier. Some daft new Irish boyband called Westlife were number one in the charts with their first single 'Swear it Again', beginning a long summer where the coveted top spot in the charts would be held almost entirely by such utter shitey excuses for artists. Two other, very different tracks were gaining traction among dance music fans by then, though. One was a simple semi-vocal trance single by a German DJ named Andre Tanneberger, otherwise known simply as ATB, the track was called 'Till I Cum' so probably wouldn't gain much commercial success, unless the track title was tweaked a little. The other track most clubbers were buzzing over was actually a bootleg mashup by an obscure artist called DJ Vimto. He had fused two tracks together; one song was 'Toca Mi' by German producers, Fragma, a largely instrumental underground track with an infectious bassline. The other song in the mashup was 'I Need a Miracle', sung by an English female vocalist using the name *Coco,* who was really called Susan Brice, famous in her own right for her work with *Way Out West, Tricky* and *Massive Attack.* 'I Need a Miracle' may have been sung and released by Coco in 1997, but it had actually been written in 1994 by Rob Davis, the former frontman of 70's glam-rock band, Mud – aye, that's right, that's right, that band who sang 'Tiger Feet', back in the day. Mashed together, these two tracks were an epic fusion of vocal house and euphoric trance, and most clubbers at the time were hooked as soon as they heard it – and dreaded the prospect of this wonderful track ever being ruined by going mainstream.

A white Peugeot 205 was speeding through the Bathgate Hills just before 10pm that night, with five passengers on board. The passengers were three guys and two lassies, all, for once, completely straight and sober – well, they'd had a few joints, but that was it.

Colin, Stevie, Kirsty, and Clare were squashed together in the new car as they had an extra passenger that evening – wee Kevin McBride. The 'other thing' that Kevin McBride had asked for in return for helping to frame Ronnie Muir was that he be allowed to meet Colin and Stevie's new pal up at Beecraigs, so he tagged along.

All were dressed to go out – the lassies in smart leggings and tops – but not heels, the lads in bog standard designer dress shirts with dark jeans.

By virtue of the fact that wee Kevin owned not only a PC but also one of those new CD writer devices, they were listening to some cutting-edge new dance music as they travelled, which Kevin had downloaded and burned onto disc from a file-sharing website called *Audio Galaxy.* To the other four passengers, the technology that had allowed Kevin to bring along this absolutely bangin' unique CD that nobody else had was near incomprehensible, no matter how many times Kev tried to explain it to them – it seemed like fuckin' magic to them – pure magic. As the new mash-up of *'I need a miracle'* and *'Toca Mi'* played, the friends chanted along in the car.

Stevie said, 'So troops, do we think this internet thing is gonnae take off, or is it just another fad, like LaserDiscs 'n' aw that pish?'

Varying opinions were mooted, but this conversation drew to an abrupt halt as the car pulled into the car park at Beecraigs just as darkness was beginning to set in. The music stopped, and the five got out of the car and headed along the track towards the picnic area and the big beech tree.

As they reached the beech tree, a face familiar to three of the party appeared in its trunk, smacking its lips and yawning, as if it had just woken up. Its big eyes rolled open.

'Jesus Christ, ye werenae lying, were yez?' said Clare, a hint of panic in her voice, but she stood firm, holding Colin's hand. Kevin just stared in awe.

'Good evening, ya bunch ae fuckin' reprobates, howdy doody?' boomed the tree, its tone almost jovial.

Stevie spoke.

'Awright mate, this is Clare, and this is Kevin, they're...'

'Ah fuckin' ken who they are, ya daftie. Hello to you, Kevin Mcbride, and hello to you, Clare Findlay. How's it hangin'?'

Kevin and Clare both answered in unison.

'How do you ken ma name?'

Colin rolled his eyes, muttering, 'Aw naw, you've done it now, this is...' but he was interrupted.

'Ah ken yer names because Ah'm a fuckin' wood fairy, an all-knowing, all-seeing, all-powerful wood fairy, that's how, teapots.'

Kevin and Clare looked stunned, but they stood still, in awe, as the tree continued.

'*Nice job ye did on that wanker of a forest ranger for me, Kevin, thanks for that, mate. A bit mare fun than wanking off at your computer wi' a bit of hash, eh pal?*'

Kevin didn't seem too embarrassed. 'Aye, a bit mate,' he said, smiling, as Kirsty, Stevie, and Colin sniggered a little. The tree then addressed Clare.

'*Hiya hen, so you're the damsel in distress, eh? Well, dinnae you worry. You've got good pals, darlin', they could've asked anything of me, but all they wanted was someone to scare away that bastard gangster of an ex of yours. For fuck's sake, what were ye daein' gawn oot wi' that fanny in the first place? Did nae cunts ever tell ye that lassies who get wet over gangsters always end up alone and bitter as fuck, usually wi' nae real pals, and wi' broken ribs and a black eye?*'

Clare answered, frankly, and calmly. She, too, had quickly accepted the talking tree as reality.

'Acht, I dinnae ken why I was wi' him. It was exciting at first, but he's a terrible person, a violent scumbag who only cares aboot himself, a pure narcissist.'

'*Ooooh, somebody swallowed a dictionary this morning, eh Clare, a narcissist? Ah've no' heard anybody use that word since ma university days.*'

'Where did you study?' asked Clare.

'*Ah studied Physiotherapy at Stirling University, then I did a postgrad in Manchester.*'

'Wow, cool,' said Clare, seeming genuinely interested.

Stevie chipped in. 'Eh, *you* were a student, really?'

'*Of course Ah wiz, why do ye ask, Stevie?*'

'It's just, well, your accent and the way you speak, you sound working class, like us, mate,' said Stevie.

Colin did a facepalm and muttered 'Aw naw, ye've done it now.'

'*What is it wi' you cunts and yer assumptions? Of course Ah went to university, why wouldn't I? Working class folk are allowed to better themselves, ye ken. Aw wait – is this you being a racist again?*'

Clare said, 'Racist? How are they being racist?'

'*Aw, they didnae tell you I'm black, did they?*'

Clare 'Eh? How are you black? You don't look black; you don't *sound* black. What do you mean?'

'Clare , please, just leave it,' pleaded Stevie, but it was too late.

'*No' another fuckin' racist. What the fuck does that mean? You believe in wood fairies but you're having trouble believing that a black guy could end up being turned into one? You think the wood fairy fraternity is the fuckin' BNP or something? I mean, wood fairies are cunts, man, but we're no' that bad. Jesus Christ. Ah dinnae sound black? How the fuck does a black guy sound, in your world? Would you prefer it if my accent conformed to your pre-conceived outdated idea of a 'black guy' voice?*'

The tree was glowing redder now and lowered two of its branches to make a 'jazz hands' gesture, before speaking in the stereotypical voice again, clearly taking the piss.

'*Hey Clare, well I am just dee wood fairy serving da masta up in the woods, you is right, masta, how could I possibly be black and educated when I gots so much cotton to pick for da boss man. Ooh lordy, is you uppa here in the forest to pick some strange fruit...*' Clare interrupted him.

'Fuck's sake, awright, awright, I'm sorry. I'm really sorry. I didnae mean to hurt your feelings, pal, I'm just stressed to the max about my ex stalking me.'

The tree wasn't impressed.

'*Well, ye did hurt ma feelings, Ah've half a mind no' tae sort oot your deranged ex now ... But a deal's a deal. Ah suppose you picked up the casual racism fae these two poofters here? I thought so.*' He waved a branch at Colin and Stevie. Clare was defiant.

'No, I'm no' a racist, neither are they, none of us are, we're ravers, man. Rave is about one love, us all being the same, any raver who is racist really doesn't fuckin' get rave culture at all. Rave and techno was started by poor working-class black people in America, it's all about unity, acceptance, and ... wait a minute, did you just call them 'poofters'?'

Clare's fiery temper was legendary, and now it was unleashed.

'They're not gay, me and Kirsty have been shagging them all week, actually. But even if they were, ye cannae call gay people that. Dinnae be such a fuckin' dinosaur, mate, this is 1999, this isnae the 1950s or an episode of fuckin' Alf Garnet.'

'*Awrite awright awright, here, I'll no' use that phrase again wi' youze, it's just banter. Sometimes at school and at uni when I was picked on for being black, I used to try to get the bullies to pick on the obvious poof ... I mean, gay guys, instead.*'

Clare was having none of it.

'It's no' just about the phrase, pal, I know your story, how ye got turned into a magic tree...'

The tree interrupted to correct her with, '*wood fairy,*' but she carried on.

'Aye, whatever. You've had a hard time, you've probably suffered racism all your life, then somebody turned you into a fuckin' wood fairy. Does that mean you have to be a loudmouth, abusive homophobic twat? My pals are gonnae help ye. We're aw gonnae help ye. But you need to help yourself, too, man.' Her tone softened.

'Look, in western culture, the last 500 years have seen the black community and the gay community persecuted, discriminated against and demonised. And do you know who's had it nearly as bad for the entirety of that time? White poor people. See, we were all at the bottom of the food chain, ken? Last in the queue, the damned, born 3–0 down in life. Racism and homophobia are the tools that rich cunts used to keep us all from uniting and demanding better lives with one voice, don't you see?'

'*Ah, well, when ye put it like that,*' the tree sounded ponderous.

Clare continued, 'You were a raver once yourself, I was told, think back to your days at the Hacienda or at they big warehouse parties, was there any discrimination there? Was there fuck. One love, man. Sweet harmony. Now, my pals say you're gonnae help us and I'm grateful if you can get this Gavin Kerr off ma back, I really am, but if you're gonnae dae this, dae it because it's the right thing to do, for fellow pillheads, for fellow ravers, or else, what was the point in all those nights you spent on the dancefloor and at parties?'

Clare lost her composure and started to cry, sinking down onto her haunches in the long summer grass, her head in her hands. It was pitch black now, the only light was the beaming red glow emanating from the tree, silhouetting the five figures around it.

Colin and Stevie had been skinning up and produced two 5-skinner joints. Kevin pulled a small joint from his shirt pocket.

The tree sat, its face twisted in a mix of anger and deep thought. Stevie lit up a joint, took a draw then stepped over and held the joint up to the tree's mouth. The tree continued staring into space, motionless, but it took two large puffs of the joint, before Stevie passed the joint to Colin. Clare was back on her feet. The tree said nothing, still, as the five visitors smoked the three joints. After a few minutes, the tree spoke.

'*Here, Colin, she's a fiery one, I bet she's some ride, eh?*'

There was a beat. Nobody could believe what the tree had just said.

Then all present, Clare included, erupted into guffaws of laughter and stoner giggles, which soon became loud belly laughs, echoing around the glade of Beecraigs Country Park.

'You're no' real, man,' said Colin to the tree, laughing still.

'*I am real, Ah'm a wood fairy, an all-powerful... nah, listen. Clare, sister, please forgive my outdated rhetoric. Your words have touched my wooden heart, Ah'm sorry Ah wound you up. It's a habit I'll try to break, Ah promise. Colin, sorry I noised up yer woman, man. Right, so, we've got a cunt to be sorting oot tonight, what time do you think he'll get here? Here, that soap bar isnae bad at all...*' The tree had 'stoner' eyes once more.

The hoot of an owl startled everyone. Down the track they saw car headlights pull into the picnic area car park.

'*Right, I need to go back undercover, dae my disappearing act, ken, but dinnae worry, I'm still here, I'm still listening, teapots,*' and with that, the tree's face vanished from its trunk, leaving them all standing in the moonlight, with a small torch on Kevin's keyring their only other light, luckily, it was summer, so it wasn't completely pitch black.

Two figures with torches were approaching.

Chapter Nineteen

Proximus

Two pairs of boots crunched heavily on the stony path, making their way through the eerie, hot, dark summer night towards the small gathering of people beside the big beech tree. These boots belonged to two men in their late 30s, both wearing long leather jackets which skirted around the back of their knees, jeans, black leather gloves and Doc Marten boots. One was a big bearish oaf with greasy hair and a permanently angry, if glaikit, expression, standing six feet and four inches tall. The other was shorter at five foot eight stocky and muscular with a freshly shaved head hiding severe male pattern baldness. They looked like gangsters. They were gangsters.

Colin, Stevie and the others could see that Kerr and Fat Carson were dressed for a fight, and a collective chill went up the spine of the five friends, after all, nobody had a clue just how the tree was going to handle this – if it was even going to handle it at all – there was no plan B.

The two gangsters came to a halt a few yards from their prospective victims, then stopped, shining their torches over them. Kerr spoke.

'Well well well, what a cheery gathering we have here. Tweedle Dee and Tweedle Dum wi' their daft wee hermit mate, and the love of ma life wi' her best mate.'

He turned to Stevie and Colin. 'So, this is your idea of a mob, is it? This is yer backup?' Kerr laughed mockingly, Fat Carson joined in laughing, like he was Muttley to Kerr's Dick Dastardly. Kerr continued, sneeringly, as the five friends stood in terror.

'A wee trip up tae Beecraigs to look at the sky at night, I never knew there were so many would-be astronomers in the fuckin' scheme. Well, they do say that West Lothian does have some of lowland Scotland's finest sites for stargazing, due to its relative lack of light pollution at night, is that no' right, Carson?' Kerr loved to play the know-it-all whenever he could, despite his middling intellect.

Carson replied on cue, 'Aye, that's right, Ah looked it up in that new internet cafe doon the centre earlier.'

Kerr continued.

'See, folks, Ah have it on good authority that you lot have been plotting ma demise, and that you cooked up some daft fuckin' strategy to lure me up here to do me in, or ye were aw gonnae meet up here and then come after me, Carson here heard you two jokers talking about it in the *Nirvana* bogs last night.'

Colin and Stevie looked at each other, seeming alarmed, which Kerr naturally picked up on.

'Oh, I see that's news to you wee fannies. Well, whatever yer plan was, it's oot the windae now, ye didnae for a minute think that Ah'd willingly come up here and pre-emptively sort you fuckers oot, did ye? See, I like to keep ma enemies guessing. So, what weapons did ye bring? Blades? Chibs?'

Stevie answered.

'Nothing, Gavin, nae weapons, they're for shitebags,'

Kerr seemed taken aback by young Stevie's courage, raising an eyebrow, furrowing his shaved head into rippled layers of skin, then he spoke again.

'Well, you've got guts, I'll give ye that. Aye, weapons are never a good solution, that's a beau geste on your part, lads. Ah take ma hat off to ye. Thing is, though, me and ma pal Carson here dinnae really believe in chivalry or any of that shite, do we, mate?' He glanced at Carson, who replied, 'Naw man, occupational necessity in our line of work.'

'That's right,' continued Kerr, as he reached into the back of his jacket and brought out a Japanese katana samurai sword, at least two feet in length, its blade shining in the moonlight. As he did, Fat Carson pulled an old sawn-off shotgun from the back of his jacket and stood in the moonlight, grinning inanely.

Colin, Stevie, Clare, Kirsty, and Kevin were aghast. Nobody had expected this. They had spent the last few days worrying about what would happen if the tree killed Kerr outright, it had never crossed their minds that it could be them who wouldn't make it out of Beecraigs alive.

Kerr, incredibly smug now, instructed the three lads to stand to one side of the tree and the two lassies to stand at the other, as he told Fat Carson to cover them with the sawn-off and his torch. Then Kerr made them all kneel.

Meanwhile, the tree did not stir.

Kerr paced back and forth in front of the terrified friends and began a monologue, like all sociopaths, he loved the sound of his own voice.

'See, Colin, Stevie, you wee fannies weren't even on ma fucking radar. You were just two wee harmless cunts fae the scheme, but then ye got in league wi' these two wee harlots here, and maybe gettin' yer dicks wet has made ye a bit brave, ken? I understand that; I really do. Pussy can make men act strangely; Ah get that. Ah even sympathise. But then, ye crossed the line, ye started plotting, making plans against me, the top dawg, the fuckin' Godfather. That scheme is *mine*. Ye crossed the line, boys, and I'm gonnae punish you for that – really punish ye.'

The colossal prick held his sword blade up to the throat of Colin, and then Stevie, in turn. They kneeled motionless, silent, as Kerr continued, resuming his pacing. He turned to Kevin.

'And as for you, a wee internet creep like you is the shite oan ma shoe, you're nothing to me, fuck all, but yer a silly boy. I'm half-inclined to let you go, from what I hear you'll probably die in some tragic wanking accident in front of your computer soon, anyway, but see, ye had to try to be the big man, ye had to come along to back up yer two wee mates, that cannae go unanswered, so, you'll be punished, too, Kevin.'

Colin thought to himself, 'This psychotic cunt sure does his homework, he knows his enemy.' Colin's train of thought was interrupted as a terrified Kevin blurted something out.

'That isn't why Ah'm up here, Mr Kerr, nobody here wants any trouble, you've been misinformed, this is aw a big misunderstanding.'

Kerr stiffened where he stood, then he replied.

'Oh really? I've been misinformed? I'm soooo so sorry. Okay, I'll just head off now and we'll forget this ever happened, sorry to have troubled you, sir.' His tone hardened.

'If there's one thing I cannae stand more than smelly wee internet hermits, it's lying smelly wee internet hermits. Nae cunt lies to me – nae cunt!'

And with that, Kerr booted Kevin full force in the face, knocking out some of his teeth and sending him sprawling backwards, Kerr stepping over his prostrate body to add several more hard kicks to the lad's ribs and head.

The other four friends made to move to aid Kevin, but a voice stopped them.

'Dinnae fuckin' hink sae,' said Fat Carson, still pointing the sawn-off shotgun and the torch at them. All four of them stayed where they were – loaded guns being pointed at you tends to make one very compliant.

Kerr stopped kicking the groaning Kevin and strode over to where Kirsty and Clare were kneeling, holding the tip of his sword blade up to Kirsty's throat as he addressed her.

'I bet this was aw your idea, ya wee skank. Always interfering, ya fuckin' fat howk, ye.'

Kirsty said nothing, she was shaking, but her eyes were fixed defiantly right on Kerr's as he continued.

'See, you've lied to me tae, multiple times, and you're probably responsible for this pathetic plot against me, too, there's no way Tweedle Dee and Tweedle Dum over there would've had the notion nor the balls to act alone. You've always been fuckin' trouble, ya wee hing-oot. You should've kept yer nose oot of other people's business, ya cunt. Now, because of your schemes, you'll all be punished tonight. Ah'll mibby even make the punishment last a bit longer. Mibby Ah'll go and pay Colin and Stevie's mums and dads a visit, me and Carson here. Maybe I'll make sure that none of ye cunts can buy drugs anywhere in the Central Belt, ever again. Or, well, ye ken how bad rumours spread, maybe Ah'll let it be known that you're all grasses and are on the smack, aye, maybe that's what Ah'll dae – nae cunt in the scheme will ever talk to ye again.'

Kerr removed the blade edge from Kirsty's throat. Clare spoke up.

'Leave them all alone, please, Gavin, your problem is with me, is it no'?'

Kerr's response was instant.

'Ah was beginning to think that cat had gotten your tongue, hen. Where's ma 1500 quid, darling?' The menace in Kerr's voice was all too clear.

'It's £500 I owe you, not £1500,' answered Clare.

BROKEN BISCUITS : THE WOOD FAIRY

'£1500, remember?' said Kerr.

'It's no' fuckin' £1500, Gavin, c'mon, man, that's two months wages,' pleaded Clare.

'Okay, then, I've no wish to sound unreasonable,' Kerr answered, sounding conciliatory, before adding 'Let's just call it a round two grand.'

'Ye cannae dae that, that's no' fuckin' fair,' said Clare.

Sneering, Kerr continued.

'Well, my love, life's no' fair, is it? What's no' fair is lassies no' paying for their drugs. What's no' fair is hearing that the former love of yer life has taken up wi' some wee pillhead fae the scheme. What definitely isn't fuckin' fair is hearing that yer ex-girlfriend has been plotting against ye, too. No, none of that's very fair at all, is it?'

Clare tried to be calm, talking in her work voice.

'When we were together you controlled me, you hit me, you manipulated me. Then, when I ended it, you stalked my steps, getting folk to spy on me, threatening my pals, threatening any guy I went with, intimidating my elderly parents, spreading lies about me. You never loved me – you just wanted to own me – that's not love.'

'Ah did fuckin' love ye,' said Kerr, losing his cool for a moment, it seemed.

Clare went on another rant.

'You're a fuckin' horrible person, Gav, you run roughshod over all the poor people in the scheme, getting their bairns addicted to drugs, ruining lives, destroying families, you're not a man – you're a fuckin' animal and I regret ever having your grubby hands on me. Colin is ten times the man you are,'

Something inside Kerr seemed to snap and he stepped over and booted Colin square in the face, Colin fell backwards, Kerr standing over him with the tip of his sword right on Colin's crotch. Kerr looked straight at

Clare, all the while, Fat Carson still had them covered with the shotgun, so nobody could fight back.

'How aboot Ah cut this wee prick's balls off? Would ye like that? Then we'll see how much of a man he is compared to me, won't we?' Kerr had now gone full psycho, and Clare knew it. With no intervention from the tree, there was only one thing she could do.'

'Gavin, look, I know that it's me you want. Let the rest of them go and I'll come back with you tonight, and we can talk. You'll get your money, I promise.'

Kerr glanced at Fat Carson, then back at Clare, exhaling, as if exhausted.

'Ok, hen, so, we just leave these freaks here, and you and me go back to my pad for a wee heart to heart, maybe sort things out, does that sound fair?'

Clare nodded, 'Aye, it's for the –' Kerr interrupted her.

'Do ye think Ah'm fuckin' buttoned up the back, ya daft cow? See, now you've lied to me as well. Ah fuckin' hate lying cows like you. Don't flatter yersel', hen, I just want ma money, Ah'm no' interested in you and yer bucket fanny anymore, you all plotted to fuck me over in some way, so, tonight you'll all be fuckin' punished. '

Kerr moved the blade away from the terrified Colin's crotch and told him to kneel again, which he did, just as a dazed Kevin got back up onto his knees, blood all around his mouth. Kerr continued, resuming his pacing.

'Ah had originally planned just to scare the shite out of you cunts tonight, but instead, you're aw gonnae fuckin' suffer. I think we'll have you aw hobble home, wounded, without your clothes. Then, when yer back in the scheme, your real punishments will begin. You'll aw wish you'd never been fuckin' born – so will yer fuckin' families. Nae cunt fucks wi' me. Get ready for a living hell. You, Colin, geez yer car keys, Loverboy.'

Everybody heard a twig snap, and then a bright, dazzling torch lit up the part of the glade where this rather nasty showdown was happening. A few yards behind Fat Carson was the silhouette of a tall figure. Nobody could see who it was because of the dazzling light. A new voice broke the darkness, as Kerr spun around. Everybody heard the unmistakable sound of a rifle being cocked.

'You, sumo, fat cunt, drop the shooter, *now!*' The voice was male, adult, emotionless.

Chapter Twenty

Not Over Yet

Fat Carson bent down and placed the sawn-off shotgun on the grass, stepping back from it when the voice told him to.

'Not one of you cunts move,' said the voice.

Kerr took orders from no cunt. 'Who the fuck are you?' he bullishly called to the figure.

The largely tranquil summer night was shattered by a deafening BANG as a high velocity .303 bullet grazed Kerr's ear, though the scumbag remained on his feet, shocked, but not so bullish anymore.

'Shut the fuck up, you, or the next one goes in yer fuckin' belly,' said the voice. Everyone heard the rifle bolt as the figure chambered another round. Nobody was moving now. The figure took a few steps closer, shining its torch along the group gathered next to the tree. The voice spoke again.

'So, I vowed to myself I would get you cunts and take ma revenge. So, who's idea was it?'

Everyone was silent for a moment, then Stevie called out, 'What idea, mate?'

The figure stepped closer, booting Fat Carson on the back of the knees and flooring him, telling him to 'stay doon', then the figure picked up the sawn-off shotgun and threw it away. The moonlight now illuminated the figure and all were aghast. Before them, stood a middle-aged man wearing jeans and a chequered shirt. He looked like a body builder and had a bushy moustache.

'Mr Muir?' blurted out wee Kevin.

The voice was angry now.

'Kevin fuckin' McBride? Ah fuckin' knew it was you, ya wee bastard. You tried to ruin ma life. Because of you I've been accused by the polis of being a beast, a pervert, an IRA supporter, a drug dealer, and a general fuckin' weirdo. Ah got suspended from my work and the wife threw me oot. You're fuckin' deed, son.'

Chapter Twenty-One

Fly Away

Ronnie Muir, the irate forest ranger who Kevin had framed as a favour to Colin and Stevie, was about to have his revenge, until he was interrupted.

'*If ye think that was bad, wait until aw the speeding fines arrive in the post, Ronnie.*'

The glade around was instantly lit up by a warm, red glow emanating from within the beech tree, upon whose trunk a friendly but gnarled face had just appeared, its red eyes, nose and mouth ablaze, its voice booming and authoritative, yet oddly jovial.

Everyone turned to look at the tree, some with relief, some with sheer terror.

'H...h...how do you know ma name?' Stuttered Muir, trembling with fear.

'*Drop the fuckin' shooter muir, drop it now.*' Muir did.

'*And you, fuckin' hard cunt, drop the fuckin' samurai.*' Aghast, a shaken Kerr did just that.

'*You lot, get off yer fuckin' knees, stand up, go on.*' The five friends rose to their feet, visibly shaken, but nonetheless relieved.

'Where the fuck have you been?' Stevie asked the tree, in an accusing tone. The tree ignored him.

'Haw you, forest ranger cunt, much as your timely intervention here was welcome, you're no' really part of the bigger picture here. See, Ah'm a wood fairy, an all-powerful, all-knowing, all-seeing entity with immense power within this wooded glade. I ken everything, see, everything. I dinnae take kindly to jobsworth fuckin' busybodies like you who come up tae ma woods spray painting things and looking to fell trees, especially no' me, so, I had these young fellas here take active measures to ensure that you weren't able to come up to chop me down on Friday there – that was the plan, right?'

Muir stammered, mesmerised, 'Aye, but erm, I promise I'll never chop you down, Mr Magic Tree...'

'Ah'm a fuckin' wood fairy.'

'Aye, sorry, Mr Wood Fairy, sir,' said Muir.

'So, Mr Forest Ranger, I dinnae actually care if you chop me down or no' anymore, in fact, next week, when you're allowed back to work and when your wife has calmed down and lets you back in the hoose and your life is back to normal, which I promise you will happen, please feel free to give me a pruning. One thing, though, there's to be no comebacks on young Kevin here, or Stevie and Colin – they were just helpin' me oot – it was nothing personal, no recriminations, are we on the same page, Mr Forest Ranger?'

Muir answered, 'Absolutely, mate, please, don't hurt me, and don't worry, I'll no' say anythin' aboot this.'

The tree laughed loudly, louder than usual, the red glow from within its trunk growing brighter, illuminating the entire glade in a warm, bright red hue.

'You'll no' say anything? What the fuck would ye say anyway, ya fuckin' teapot? A respectable person would have trouble enough convincing anybody they'd encountered a talking magic tree up Beecraigs, so what chance has a suspected terrorist-loving beast, drug-dealing, philandering pervert got of being believed? They'll put ye in the fuckin' mad hoose. And, if Ah ever find

out that you've broken our arrangement and have come after these three lads, or tried to sell yer story to the fuckin' Daily Sport or the Discovery Channel or any ae that shite, I'll get ye, capiche?'

Muir nodded and sheepishly asked, 'Can I go now, please?'

'*Aye, go on, fuck off, teapot. Leave the shooter.*'

And with that, Ronnie Muir was gone. He had shat himself during the chat with the tree. Literally. He squelched back to his borrowed car, borrowed from the same uncle in Stoneyburn who had loaned him the hunting rifle. With shite running down the back of his legs he drove off, humiliated again.

Those remaining around the tree breathed a sigh of relief, then came the night's second loud BANG.

Chapter Twenty-Two

Take The Long Way Home

Fat Carson had taken advantage of the tree being preoccupied with Muir and had rolled his flabby frame along the ground to grab the sawn-off shotgun, aimed it at the trunk of the tree and pulled both triggers. Miraculously, none of the pellets struck a human being. One did strike the tree on the nose, but the damage was minimal. The tree turned to Fat Carson, who was fumbling to reload the weapon, his hands shaking.

'Listen you, ya big tub of lard, you were actually gonnae be walking away fae this one unscathed, but you just took a liberty, ya cunt. Say adios, sumo.'

One of the tree's long branches sprung forward and curled itself around Carson's considerable midriff, lifting him off the ground. As Carson begged and whimpered to be set free, the tree started to swing him around and around in a circle above its head, spinning him faster and faster, higher and higher, the fat gangster's whimpers becoming terrified, deafening screams which filled the night sky. Carson soon became a flabby blur against the night sky. Everyone wondered what the tree would do next.

As the fat, greasy thug was twirled around in the air by the tree's branch, the tree spoke to Carson, warmly reminiscing, as the leg breaker squealed like a pig.

'See, Carson, Ah miss a lot aboot life, having been stuck in this fuckin' tree this last decade, but ken what I miss the most? When yer young and hangin'

aboot wi' yer friends, clubbing, partying, shagging, living, ye can fly. Allow me to explain. One minute, ye can aw be sittin' in yer mate's gaff drinking a few beers and having a smoke, then, hallelujah, one of ye suggests goin' oot tae a club. Ye aw run aboot mad, gettin' ready, ironing clothes, checking yer hair's no' a pure riot, puttin' better tunes on, ye maybe call a taxi, or phone up to check the bus times, then, within an hour, maybe less, you can be under the disco lights, havin' it large with a thousand other young, beautiful, happy people – they all flew, too. One minute, ye were having a quiet one, then you flew, and as quick as a flash, you and yer pals were all on another planet, immersed in pure hedonism. Together, you fly all night together like a whirlwind, you fly hame tae, and six hours or so later, after the afterparty, when it's just you and yer mates chilling oot before you all pass out, you look back on the night and ye realise – we can fly. A lot of the time, folk dinnae realise that they can fly, until they stop goin' oot as much, or stop altogether. That's when it hits ye – when you're young, ye can fuckin' fly. Is this makin' sense to you, Mr Carson?'

Carson continued squealing and screaming as he zoomed around in ever quickening circles above the tree, the tree taking care not to injure him as he spun. The tree continued as if Fat Carson had answered coherently.

'Naw, I don't suppose you would, Carson. Being little more than that Kerr's gofer and pathetic enforcer backup gimp, I don't suppose you've got the faintest idea what Ah'm talkin' aboot, eh? I mean, you're probably nae stranger to drugs, pubs and clubs, and dodgy parties, ye've maybe even pumped yer fair share of drunk lassies, junkie birds, and hookers, but, let's face it, Carson, you've no' made any real friends due to your dreadful life choices, have ye? No E-fuelled hugs on the dancefloor from strangers for you, eh? No euphoric weekends to remember? Nae cunt is ever pleased to see you, are they, ya cunt?'

The tree continued spinning the squealing Carson above its canopy as it turned to address Colin, Stevie, Kirsty, Clare, and wee Kevin.

'*See, that's why Ah love you, cunts. Youze are good cunts. Ye never ran away in terror from the scary talking tree, ye never judged me about how Ah ended up like this, you took me as you found me, you accepted me. Nae bullshit, nae grovelling, nae asking for things for personal gain – except that fitba score, he he he – all you wanted from me was my help eradicating your scumbag problem, and you offered to help me, tae. Dae ye ken what Ah mean aboot the flying? Ah reckon you guys fly all the time, and dinnae even realise it.*'

Stevie answered first. 'Aye, mate, Ah know what ye mean. We fly, man, we fly.'

Kirsty added, 'Fuckin' sure we can fly, mate, we're a pure weekend flying squadron.'

Clare, in a more sombre tone, said 'Aye, man, we fly.'

Colin said, 'We'll never stop flyin', mate.'

Wee Kev even piped up, 'Ah used to love flying wi' these guys, maybe one day I will again. That's what it is, you're right, man, friends fly together.'

Stevie continued, 'You're our mate now, man, one of the gang – one of us. Remember, we're ravers – acceptance is our kinda thing.'

The face on the tree seemed to soften its gnarled, permanently-a-bit-annoyed expression. A drop of water welled up in one of its eyes, then rolled down its face, falling off the bark and splashing to the ground. The tree smiled at the friends, but then quickly realised it was still swinging a thug around in the air with its branches. '*Hold on the now,*' he said to the friends.

'*Right, Carson, that's enough ae you, Ah fuckin' hate guns, by the way – go on, fuck off,*' boomed the tree, before releasing Carson, sending him flying at lightning speed through the West Lothian night sky, to the south-east.

Carson's screams were audible for a full thirty seconds before they faded away, as the fat bastard rocketed off into the abyss of night.

'Fuckin' hell, man,' blurted out an amazed Stevie. The five friends were all standing together now, their terror and anxiety having completely abated. The tree spoke again, much more harshly.

'Haw you, get back here.'

Kerr had taken advantage of the others' distraction to try and make a run for it, his ear still bleeding from the gunshot wound. However, he hadn't been able to resist picking up the forest ranger's discarded rifle en route, anything to try and regain his sense of control of the situation. That momentary pause allowed the tree to whip out another one of its branches and wrap itself around Kerr's ankle, tugging him to the ground. He fell with a thud, holding the rifle tightly as he was quickly dragged along the grass until he lay helpless at the feet of the five young people he had, only moments earlier, been about to maim and humiliate. No sooner had he come to a halt than Colin snatched the rifle from him, clearing the bullet from its chamber – he'd seen that done in *Saving Private Ryan*.

The friends looked down at their tormentor. It was only then that they realised – without access to his hoodlums, his backup, weapons, money, drugs, and the scheme itself, he wasn't really much at all – just a well-built, balding man in his late 30s. Pathetic, really.

The tree's branch remained tightly wrapped around Kerr's ankle – he wasn't getting up or going anywhere.

Kirsty was the next to speak.

'So, folks, what are we gonnae dae wi' this cunt?'

'Here, Kevin, why don't you go and skin up on they benches there?' said the tree.

'Aye, shhurre, nae bother,' said Kevin, through bloody, broken teeth.

'*Build two five-skinners,*' snapped the tree. Soon Kevin was rolling two joints amid the vibrant red glow of the tree, which still filled the glade.

It didn't take Kevin long to finish rolling – all that time spent stoned alone as a chain-wanking porn-addicted internet hermit had finally come in useful, it seemed.

The friends stood in blissful silence for a few moments, each taking their turn on the joints. Soon, all were stoned, including the tree, whose eyes were now their trademark bloodshot once again. The tree also now had a bit of a smoker's cough. After one particularly loud coughing burst which shook the very ground on which they stood, it spoke again.

Chapter Twenty-Three

Café Del Mar

'Kirsty, tae answer yer question, what we are gonnae dae wi' this cunt – Ah'm afraid that's no' really your call, that's ma call. Y'see, Ah'm a wood fairy, and ...'

'Aye, aye, aye, heard it,' blurted out Colin, interrupting him. Everybody except Kerr giggled.

'Fuck off, Colin, this is serious. Ah'm a wood fairy, all-powerful, all-knowing, I see the bigger picture, ken what Ah mean?' It continued. 'This fucker lying here is now ma responsibility. Kerr. Gavin Kerr, we've met before, a long time ago, obviously before I got trapped in this tree. Do you mind of me?'

Kerr was frightened but also angry – his ego battling his common sense at the worst of all possible times.

'Naw, I've never met you before, I've never done you any wrong before, and you've never done me any, either. Well done, you've succeeded in putting the frighteners on me, though. Look, just tell me what yez want? I don't want to end up like Carson, so tell me what you all want, and we can end this daft game here and now.'

'Yer fat mate's no' deed,' said the tree.

'Fuck off, you hurled him away like a piece of rubbish.'

'That's what he wiz, Ah mean, is,' the tree interrupted him, half laughing, before continuing.

'See, as an all-powerful wood fairy, I know everything. No' just folk's business, but all things aboot science, art, maths, history, the fuckin' lot.'

'Aye ... so?' asked Kerr, more sheepishly.

'So, right now, your mate, Fat Carson, is lying face down in a huge pile of manure, in a cow field near Mid Calder – bruised, scared, covered from head to toe in shite, but basically fine. That is, of course, unless I fucked up my angle and trajectory when I tossed him, in which case, he would be splatted like a giant lard pizza against the side of that huge Cameron Iron Works factory in Livingston. But, as trigonometry and physics are well within the remit of us wood fairies, Ah'm certain it's the former.'

'Bullshit,' said Kerr. 'How could you know that?'

'Ah know that because Ah'm a fuckin' wood fairy and Ah know everything, ya cunt! Less of the attitude from you, ya piece of shit, or you'll be next. Maybe I'll bounce ye off the Forth Bridge? Maybe I'll splat ye off the side of the New Lanark mill? Choices, choices ... what about you guys, any suggestions?'

Clare said, 'Drown him in the Forth.'

Stevie said, 'Just tear him limb from limb, mate.'

Colin said, 'Toss him towards ICI at Grangemouth – naw wait, ma da works there and–'

'Fuck's sake, Colin,' interrupted the tree, shaking its face disapprovingly. *'What about you, Kirsty?'*

'Well, whatever we decide to do with him, it has to be permanent, cos this cunt doesn't know the meaning of forgiveness and ye cannae trust a word he says. If we don't get this right he'll come after us all, one by one, he'll get us all. He'll probably fuckin' kill us.'

'Answer yer phone,' the tree said to Kerr, who looked puzzled.

Then, a strange sound was heard by all. It was a really annoying bleeping sound, coming from Kerr's jacket pocket. Kerr took a device out of his pocket. It was slightly smaller than a SKY TV remote control and had a pointy plastic protrusion on one end – it was one of those new mobile phone things.

The Nokia ringtone bleeped irritatingly before Kerr answered the call, nervously.

'Woah, are you awright? Really? Mid Calder? No, Ah cannae come and pick ye up, ya fat bastard. You'll need to walk it. Look, mate, I really need you to...'

Another gnarled branch crept out from the tree and snaked its way around Kerr's neck, causing him to pause mid-sentence. The tree spoke in a hushed whisper, inaudible to the primitive audio system of the mobile phone.

'*Tell him you're alright and that you're away to Glasgow for a few days, and that if he ever repeats this story to any cunt, he's a dead man. Oh aye, and tell him all is good wi' the boys and girls here, all sorted oot amicably.*'

As the branch around his neck tightened slightly, not enough to restrict his breathing but enough to send a clear message that any deviation from the tree's instructions would result in instant asphyxiation, Kerr told Fat Carson just that, then ended the call.

'*Thank you, Gavin,*' said the tree, politely. The branch around Kerr's neck slipped off and snatched the chunky Nokia mobile phone from Kerr's hand, then crushed it almost flat, before slipping it into the tree's mouth. The tree chewed and swallowed the small lump of plastic, burping and then smiling.

'*See, Mr Kerr, things can always be resolved amicably, with a bit of good will.*'

BROKEN BISCUITS : THE WOOD FAIRY

The cheeky bastard, Kerr, then said, 'Right, so, can I go now? Lesson learned. Ah'll head through to Glasgow, like you said, and I'll no' give this lot any more hassle, I promise, you have my word. Besides, if you do anything bad to me here, Carson will be the last person to have seen me alive, he'll go to the cops. You'll aw get the jail for joint enterprise, and ye know it. What we have here, folks, is a draw. So, can I go?'

'Wait a minute, we haven't asked young Kevin here what he thinks we should dae wi' you, yet.'

Kerr was getting cockier, sensing that he might just be able to talk his way out of this, after all, then hunt them all down afterwards.

'What the fuck's it got to do wi' him?' asked Kerr aloud.

'You kicked him in the fuckin' chops that's what it's got to dae wi' him,' snapped the tree.

Kevin piped up.

'Look, I did my bit to help with this mental situation, and I got to see the magic tree...'

'Ah'm a fuckin' wood fairy, how many times, ya fuckin' teapots!'

'Aye, sorry, I got to meet the wood fairy. I just want there to be nae mare hassle for my mates or me, and I want Kerr to promise to leave us all alone and to forget about that money he says Clare owes him,' said Kevin, calmly. His mouth had stopped bleeding.

A clamour of indistinct, angry objecting chatter from Stevie, Colin and the others greeted that statement, but the tree quickly shushed them.

'Well, Gavin, are those terms acceptable tae you?'

Kerr really couldn't believe his luck. He was going to walk away from this, in one piece. These wee scumbags and their fuckin' magic tree had had their chance to get rid of him and blown it. Kerr tried his best to sound contrite and magnanimous – which isn't easy if you're a small-time mobster piece of shite with no respect for anybody.

'Look, we've all said and done things that we regret, let's just pretend that all this never happened. I'll just be on my way. No recriminations, I give you my word. So, aye, I accept your terms.'

'Oh wait, one thing, though, Gavin. Nobody's asked me what Ah think we should dae wi' you.'

Kerr said, 'What *do* you want done wi' me? Mind, you and I have no beef with each other, no history at all, pal.'

'*Oh, have we no?*' boomed the tree. '*Are ye sure about that, Mr Kerr?*' The tree's tone had a menacing edge.

'Ah think I'd have remembered meeting a talking tr... erm I mean a wood fairy, pal,' said Kerr, trying to sound friendly.

'*Oh aye, cos Ah've always been a fuckin' wood fairy, eh?*'

'What do ye mean?' asked Kerr, nervously.

'*Cast your mind back to 1989, Gavin, the summer of love, do you remember those heady days? Ah dae, like they were yesterday.*'

'Long time ago, pal,' said Kerr, still nervous but trying to appear relaxed, much to the annoyance of the five friends.

'*Well, permit me to refresh your memory a little. It's May 1989. You were still an up-and-coming right-hand man for some drug dealer scumbag. You're at a party in Glasgow, a big do, in some cunt's big garden in Milngavie. You had some of yer wee minions in tow, in fact, you were supplying the eccies. At this party, you tried it on with a tidy young Manc lassie outside the bog in the hoose. She knocked ye back and managed to get away fae ye. Yer pathetic ego was so bruised that you went ootside and picked a fight wi' her boyfriend, you smacked him one, his mate booted you in the baws, you were gonnae stab them but yer creepy wee mates talked you out of it, then the party hosts made you leave by threatening to phone yer boss to complain – does that ring any bells?*'

'Nah, wiznae me, I've never been at a party in Milngavie, you must have me confused with somebody else, pal.' said Kerr.

'*Ah'm no' yer fuckin' pal,*' barked the tree.

'Aye, sorry, sorry, you're the man, what you say goes. But I was never at a party in Milngavie.'

'*You're a fuckin' grass, Gavin, a dirty fuckin' rat, aren't ye?*'

Kerr seemed annoyed by that.

'Ah'm never a fuckin' grass, Ah'd never dae that. I operate outside the law.'

'*Bullshit. Yer a grass. A snake.*'

'Eh? Ah'm no' a grass. How am I a grass? I wouldn't even give the polis the time of day, man.'

'*See, Gavin, you think that you and yer daft fat mate who went into orbit earlier are here tonight because of yer ex, Clare, and her pals, and some hare-brained scheme they've cooked up. The truth is, you're here because of me, just like I'm here because of you, ya cunt.*'

'But I've never met you before, honest, man, mistaken identity.'

Kerr was beginning to sound rattled.

'*You're sayin' Ah'm wrong?*'

'Aye, man.'

'*You're accusing an all-powerful, all-knowing wood fairy of no' quite having his facts in order? Fuck's sake, Ah've heard it aw noo.*'

'Well, aye, but naw, I mean, c'mon man, what is this?'

'*Gavin Kerr, you were at a garden party in Milngavie in 1989. You did accost some guy's bird and then try to start a fight with her fella, as revenge for her spurning yer advances. You punched her boyfriend, Blair, then were booted square in the baws by his mate, Sandy. You considered knifing them but were then made to leave the gathering. Then, knowing that the guy who had scudded ye in the love spuds and humiliated you in front of all they cool people was heading through to a secret outdoor rave at Blackford Quarry in Edinburgh that night, a gathering that you had just been told to stay the fuck away from, one that most of the other Milngavie partygoers were also going to, you thought you'd a be a wise cunt so ye phoned up the polis and gave them an anonymous tip off about large quantities of drugs being carried along the M8 to Edinburgh, in a convoy of cars leaving from a certain address in Milngavie. Strathclyde police drugs squad had fuck-all better to do that day, so they pounced on your tip off and followed said cars.*

One car broke away from the convoy at the Bathgate junction but was still followed by the polis. It evaded the polis for a time by driving up into the Bathgate hills, where the driver and passengers abandoned the car to evade the polis and split up. One of that party ran into Beecraigs country park, where he was subsequently tricked by a wood fairy and ended up trapped inside a tree for ten fuckin' years. Blessed with power and all-seeing knowledge but trapped inside the tree and unable to leave this glade, the tree, or fuckin' wood fairy, had a lot of time to plot its revenge and it never forgot your fuckin' name. It bided its time until one night when it appeared in front of two young clubbers who were up the woods to clear their heeds after a heavy weekend. The wood fairy, being all-knowing and all-fucking-powerful, knew that these two lads were also going to be in a spot of bother, because of you, they knew you, they were sound to me and, voila, I had a way to get ye back, ya cunt.

Ye see, Gavin, though I'm all-powerful and all-knowing I can only appear as I do now, at night. I have immense powers, powers beyond your fuckin' comprehension, but only within this glade, and as Ah'm stuck inside a bloody tree, leaving the glade isn't an option, either. So, my new friendship wi' these likable pillheads also provided me with a means to actually get you up here, and you walked straight intae ma fuckin' trap, ya daft cunt. So, here ye are, before me, trembling, at ma mercy. And ken what's really funny? If you'd just been an ordinary drug-dealing lowlife and had left these good young people here alone, and maybe been a better fuckin' person, you wouldnae be here tonight – you've been entrapped by yer own hubris, ya cunt. Ya dirty cunt. Ya grassin' cunt. You grassed on us to try and punish us for showing you up in Milngavie. Well, now it's your turn for punishment, fanny baws!'

Kerr hesitated, stunned, knowing shit had just got real.

'Wait a minute, woah, so, who were you at the party in Milngavie?'

'Take a guess, smart cunt,' boomed the tree.

'Ah cannae. I can't place your voice; it was a long time ago…'

'Ah thought you said you werenae fuckin' there? Are you lying tae me? Don't you fuckin' lie to me, cunt.'

Kerr held his hand up to his mouth and looked up to the night sky, gently clicking his lips, as if trying to remember something.

'Look, mate…'

'Ah telt ye, Ah'm no' yer fuckin' mate.'

'Sorry, man. Look, I'm sorry if I was out of order at a party and annoyed ye, but I never grassed on ye, I swear,' said Kerr.

'Aye ye fuckin' did. Ah'm a wood fairy, Ah know ye did. Deny it again and I'll tear you to shreds wi' ma branches and feed ye to the fuckin' badgers.'

Kerr was, by now, genuinely puzzled, and terrified.

'Please, tell me your name, big man, let's sort this oot calmly.'

'Ma name's Sandy.'

'Sandy? I can't remember a Sandy, tell me something that'll jog ma memory, please.'

'Dinnae think yer talkin' yer way oot ae this one, cunt,' the tree said, menacingly, but then its voice softened to a more friendly tone.

'Aw come on, Gavin. Sandy, Blair's mate, the Sandy who booted ye in the baws. Ye must remember.'

Kerr looked at the ground, sighed, then looked up and spoke.

'You can't be *that* Sandy. The guy who booted me in the baws that day was a darkie-laddie. He was black.'

'*Aye, cunt, it was me, Ah booted ye in the baws, so you grassed me in, thus beginning the tragic series of events that got me stuck in this tree, and that brought you here tonight. It was me. I'm the black guy.*'

Kerr replied, 'No way, you don't sound black.'

Chapter Twenty-Four

Strange World

The tree glowed redder than ever before. Beecraigs Country Park was awash with bright red light, illuminating all around as far as the eyes could see; animals on the forest floor stirred and gathered around the picnic area, watching. Badgers, moles, squirrels, and even a wildcat sat watching the show, as if they were at the fuckin' cinema. The tree's eyes, with furrowed brows, glowed with a menace that burned like the fiery depths of Dante's Inferno. The tree's voice boomed louder and with more echo than ever before, its very breath almost knocking Kerr over as it roared.

'*Ah dinnae sound black? What the fuck does that mean? Aaaaaaaaarrrrrgggggghhhhhhhh!*'

Enraged, the tree lashed out with two of its big branches, forming fists at the tips, unleashing two murderous punches one after the other. The first branch punched Kerr right in the balls, causing him to double over in agony. The second branch then hit Kerr's jaw with a ferocious uppercut, sending him flying backwards, knocking out several teeth. Kerr got up and tried to run away, but the other branch, still wrapped around his ankle, yanked him back into exactly the same spot.

'*You're goin' nowhere, ya cunt,*' boomed the tree.

One branch then punched Kerr hard, in the stomach, completely winding him, then, as Kerr gasped for air, the other branch repeated the uppercut, sending him flying backwards once more, knocking out more teeth. Kerr lay on the ground moaning and didn't try to rise. More branches appeared from the tree canopy and snaked their way towards Kerr. Two of them pulled him over onto his back, while two other branches, each with their tips curled into what looked like fists, pounded on Kerr's legs, starting at his ankles, breaking them, then moving up to shatter his knees. Colin, Stevie, Kirsty, Clare, and Kev winced as they heard his knees crack, but remained silent, watching their tormentor take a beating, as they bathed in the warm red glow from the tree.

Kerr was now a whimpering, terrified mess lying on the grass, prostrate and helpless. Next, the branches rolled him onto his side and yanked hard, pulling his hips in opposite directions, dislocating them with a *crunch*, then the branches hammered hard on his pelvis, breaking it, shattering it, as Kerr's pleas became desperate shrieks of pain. The branches pulled Kerr across the ground, closer to the tree, increasing his excruciating agony, his howls of anguish reverberating around the illuminated glade. Then the branches began to hammer down the way, hard, on Kerr's ribs, cracking them, breaking them, like a hydraulic press shattering a ming vase. Kerr's face was twisted and agonised, his body smashed to bits from the chest down. Then, the branches stopped, and all retreated back into the canopy of the tree, all except the one still wrapped tightly around Kerr's ankle. The tree spoke to its gathered audience.

'*No' so hard now, eh Gavin? You're hurting in places you didn't even know existed until now. I'm no' a violent wood fairy, per se, Gavin, but Ah hate bullies, Ah hate racists and Ah fuckin' hate grasses. So, did ye enjoy that? Would ye like some more?*'

Kerr groaned, murmuring, 'Please, no, I'm sorry, I dinnae want to die, no' me, please.'

'Naw, Ah suppose you don't, do ye? you've got a wee drug empire to live for, eh? Ya fuckin' fanny. Real men help their community, they dinnae fuckin' destroy it, like you dae. Ya fuckin' parasite. Oh, but dinnae worry, these wounds aren't fatal, well, as long as you can get to a hospital fairly soon anyway. See, as an all-knowing wood fairy, I'm an expert on anatomy, and on medieval fuckin' torture. I could keep you alive for fuckin' days in abject agony, without even knockin' ye oot. That would serve you right, ya cunt, for aw the lives you ruin, for all the lives your ilk ruin, but we don't need to be doin' that, do we?'

The tree's tone softened again.

'As you said, this can all be sorted out calmly, can it no'?

Let's make a new deal. I'll no' hurt ye again, I'll just tell ye a few wee tales aboot this wood fairy lark, if yer interested, like, are ye interested? Shall I tell you them, then get these youngsters to dump you doon at accident and emergency? Or would you prefer it if I break the rest of yer bones then throw ye out to fuckin' sea, where, of course, you'll drown, being unable to swim because you've had yer cunt kicked in by me. So, what's it to be, do you want the stories and the hospital, or more beatings and then a watery fuckin' grave?'

Stevie butted in 'Hospital? Fuck that, we cannae take him doon there, mate, the police will ...'

'Shut it, Stevie, you and Colin go and skin up, now!'

Stevie seemed frantic 'C'mon man, we...'

'Ah said fuckin' skin up, teapots.' The tree seemed annoyed by his protests, so Stevie and Colin went to roll joints on the benches. The tree continued.

'So, Mr Gavin Kerr, what's it to be, do you want to learn, or do you want to die?'

Kerr, a pathetic mess lying on the grass, blood pouring from his mouth, had regained his breath a bit, enough to reply.

'The stories, tell me it all. Then the hospital. Tell me, tell me.'

'*Superb, Gavin, so, to be clear, do you want to know everything?*'

'Aye, m-m-man, Ah dae.'

'*Fuckin' say it then!*'

'I want to know everything.'

'*Ah-ha, but do ye, though? Do ye want to know everything? Say it again, cunt, go on.*'

'Ah just d-did, m-man.'

'*Fuckin' say it!*'

'I want to know everything.'

'*Good, now, say it one more time, go on. Or I'll rip yer fuckin' baws off.*'

Kerr hesitated. 'Why do I need to say it again, m-man?'

The tree was growing impatient '*Just fuckin' say it, now! One more time!*'

Kerr, gurgling blood, became defiant, his mumbles louder.

'Fuck you, fuck you all. You've probably crippled me for life. Ah read books as a wean, if I say that thing a third time something bad will happen, a spell or something, fuck knows, whatever, Ah'm no' sayin' it again.'

Clare paced forward then took a knee next to Kerr's head. She looked down at his broken body. Then, she looked deeply into Kerr's eyes and gently stroked his face with her finger. Her expression was warm, loving, even. Kerr seemed to relax a little, he looked straight back into her eyes. Clare spoke.

'It'll be alright, Gav, just let the tree have his wee win by making you say it three times, then we'll take you to the hospital, I promise. I'll even sit with ye at the hospital, for as long as it takes. This is a new start for us all. Just say it, Gav, everything will be alright, I promise. She then kissed his forehead.

Kerr, not fatally wounded but a frightful mess nonetheless, deliriously acquiesced to the request made by the soft voice of the young, beautiful woman that he had once loved, albeit in his own, twisted way.

'I want to know everything.'

'*Ya fuckin' dancer!*' boomed the tree, like an excited man whose horse had just won its race at a canter.

In a flash of blinding white light, Gavin Kerr, drug dealer, gangster, informer, exploiter, profiteer of others' pain, traitor to both his class and to his community, the scourge of the schemes was nowhere to be seen.

Colin, Stevie, and the rest had watched the final confrontation between the tree and Kerr with a mixture of wonder and terror – wonder at the spectacle that they had just witnessed, fear of the savagery that the tree had displayed – an aspect to the tree's nature that they'd never expected to encounter, nor ever wanted to again.

As the blinding white flash of light faded, the tree was still illuminating the glade with that eerie yet mellow, brilliant red glow, all around was red.

The small group of woodland creatures who had gathered to watch that final showdown – the wildcat, the badgers, the squirrels and the moles – giggled together in a high pitch and gave a little round of applause, before scattering in half a dozen different directions, back into the trees.

The five friends were aghast to see that the tree's face was gone, all that was there on its trunk now was bark, though the red glow continued to shine. There was no sign of Kerr, either, save for some flattened sections of grass where he had lain to take the tree's punishment.

Stevie let out a long, relieved sigh. 'Fuckin' hell, troops, well, that was one to tell the grandkids about one day, eh? Pure twilight zone.'

Before anyone could reply, they were all illuminated by the beam from a very powerful torch. A strong, intimidating Glaswegian male accent spoke to them from behind its dazzling beam.

'Funny you should mention that, Stevie.'

'Who the fuck is that?' answered Stevie, who, like the others, had had quite enough of surprise interventions for one night.

The torch dazzling the group of friends clicked off, and suddenly, in the glowing red light of the glade, they could all see clearly.

Before them, holding what had been Fat Carson's torch, was a handsome black man in his late 30s, smiling, wearing baggy flared jeans, a white *Moschino* tee-shirt and a pair of brown *Pony* trainers that looked like dress shoes. He introduced himself.

Chapter Twenty-Five

Manumission

'Awright, I'm Sandy – sorry, this must be a bit of a shock for you lot, seeing me without my branches and shit. Erm, are there any joints going?'

They all stared open-mouthed at the new arrival, before Colin answered.

'Aye, of course, mate, here, fill yer boots.' Colin had just sparked up one of the joints that the tree had asked them to build earlier, he took a puff, then gestured to Sandy to come and take it.

Sandy took the joint and took several long, deep draws on it, saying nothing, looking around, while Clare and Kirsty got started on smoking the other joint. Sandy spoke again.

'Well guys, we did it. You have set me free. Thank you, from the bottom of my heart. I feel at peace, relieved, emancipated. Wow, I thought I'd feel ill or groggy or something when I escaped, but, well, wow, thank you. Here, that soap bar's actually no' bad, by the way!'

Everybody laughed. Kirsty spoke first.

'How do you feel, mate, are you alright? I mean, do ye feel like a tree still or do you just feel like you're a guy?'

'Fuckin' hell, oh my god, that's right, I was under some sort of spell, wasn't I? Hmmmm.' Sandy paused for a moment, then spoke again.

'I don't remember much about the whole tree thing, I mean, I know I was one, I know you guys helped me to stop being one, I remember having a fight with some cunt who stitched me up years ago and ... oooh yeah. Hahahahaha. Kerr, Gavin Kerr. Classic.' Sandy sounded super relaxed, as though reminiscing about old school times.

Stevie asked, 'Aye, so where is Kerr now? Is he deed?'

Sandy was laughing 'Oh that cunt Kerr? He's in there, now. We won't be hearing from him for a long time, if at all. He's no' deed, no, he's just, well, a tree, now.' Sandy gestured towards the glowing red tree with both hands, as if saying 'ta-dah!'.

'Is that no' dangerous him being in there, Sandy? Him having all those powers you had?' asked Clare.

Sandy was dismissive. 'Well, yeah, a bit, but also nah, at least, no' right now. He'll be a bit disorientated for a few hours, I was, too, I mean, wouldn't you be, if some crafty bastard had just tricked you into being trapped inside an enchanted tree?'

'It's a wood fairy,' boomed Stevie.

All present laughed their heads off at that remark. Sandy continued.

'Nah, look, as long as we all leave here soon and don't come up here at night ever again, I reckon we're cool. He won't be cool, he'll be fuckin' raging, but that's his problem. What time is it, guys?'

Kevin said that it was 1am. Sandy was upbeat and continued.

'Well, folks, the logical conclusion to this whole, wonderful, beautiful, meaningful, memorable episode would be if we all went oot and got absolutely trashed and danced our arses off, wouldn't it, no?'

Kirsty said, 'If it's 1am we've missed the curfew for *Room at the Top* in Bathgate, and *Nirvana*, and every other venue in Scotland, man. Besides, there's six of us, now, we cannae all fit in Colin's car to get doon there.'

Sandy was adamant. 'I've just escaped from a ten-year stretch inside a beech tree, I think I can handle a short drive sitting in the boot of a Peugeot 205 – if it means goin' oot wi' you guys, that is.'

'What about Kerr's motor?' Asked Colin.

'Nah, fuck that, man,' answered Sandy. 'We don't want any fingerprints left in the car of a missing person. C'mon, you lot, let's go.'

Clare said, 'Fuck it, aye let's try and get into the *RATT,* let's have it large.'

'Magic,' said Sandy, adding, 'one thing though, hen, you and Kirsty will need to caw canny the night, and for a while actually, take it easy, I mean.'

'Eh? Why the fuck would we both dae that?' answered Clare, in happy defiance, puffing hard on the joint between her fingers, the weight on her shoulders having soared into the distance with Kerr's departure.

'Erm, look, I've already forgotten most of what it was like being a fuckin' wood fairy, but before you set me free, I had one last revelation – youze are both pregnant – as of this morning – and Colin, Stevie, aye, you're the daddies. Congratulations to ye all.'

'WHIT?' said Clare and Kirsty, in unison. 'How can ye be so sure?' asked Kirsty.

'Really? Ye really have tae ask how I knew, are you serious? I knew because I was an all-powerful…'

'Fuck off,' laughed Kirsty and Clare, together with one voice, Clare adding. 'Aye, aye, a wood fairy, we remember, heard it, mate.'

All six of them erupted into laughter as they trudged over the track, back to the car park and Colin's motor.

As they all sat crammed into the wee Peugeot 205 en route down to Bathgate, the car stereo was playing Beat 106 FM, but it wasn't blaring, as the friends had a conversation about how four of them were soon to become parents. It was a surprisingly deep, plain-speaking chat about how the arrival of children always turns hardened clubbers into stay-at-home pussies, but also about the rewards of parenthood and responsibility and how they were usually more than ample compensation for retiring from the dancefloor.

That fucking soul-destroying chat lasted barely five minutes, and if you think I'm going to waste my time transcribing that particular philosophical discourse, then, well, you've no' really been paying attention, at all. Boak.

Colin's wee car parked up outside Room at the Top in its massive car park – which was the former site of Bathgate's once thriving Friday open-air market, where once upon a time, hard-pressed locals in the desolate, poverty-stricken economic wasteland that was Thatcher's Britain, would gather to buy cut-price counterfeit designer clothes, counterfeit chart albums, sectarian racist flute band tapes – green and blue- unidentifiable cuts of meat from a mobile E-Coli butcher van, Naff Naff t-shirts, white sports socks – the greatest fashion crime of the 20th century – and knock-off cigarettes and rolling tobacco, all washed down with a Styrofoam cup of tea and a manky roll an' sausage from a van, guaranteed to give you the shits.

The six pals headed for the club's main entrance, there was no queue because it was so late. They could feel the bass reverberating through the air, making their insides shake. The song 'Communication' by Mario Pui was pumpin', filling the West Lothian night sky for a mile around.

Somebody answer the phone
Somebody answer the phone
Somebody answer the phone
Somebody answer the phone
Somebody answer the phone
Somebody answer the phone
Somebody answer the phone

Somebody answer the phone

There were just two bouncers guarding the entrance to West Lothian's superclub. One was a large, pot-bellied, baldy guy in his 40s, with a moustache, the other was a well-built, strong but pretty-looking woman with dark hair. Both wore colourful uniforms under long black coats. As the friends reached the club's steps, the baldy bouncer held out his hand in a 'stop' gesture and said, 'Sorry, guys, no' the night, yer a bit late.' He actually sounded a bit apologetic and chilled, though firm.

'Aw come on, man,' pleaded Stevie.

'Naw, sorry,' said the bouncer.

'But we've both just found out we're pregnant,' blurted out Kirsty.

The bouncer smiled. 'Oh really, wow, that's brilliant. Congratulations to ye both. So, who are the lucky guys?'

Colin and Stevie both held up a hand apiece, smiling. They weren't used to facing nightclub bouncers when basically sober. Usually, when encountering a bouncer on a big night, most clubbers, fuckin' wrecked already on drink and sometimes drugs, too, had to master the 'sober for 30 seconds routine', in order to gain entry and not face the humiliation of getting a knockback. However, that wasn't necessary on this particular evening, as only a small amount of weed had been consumed by all.

The bouncer shook Colin's, and then Stevie's hand in congratulations, then added

'Delighted for ye guys, I recognise you all, you're good folk, never any bother. I wish you every happiness.'

'So, we can get in?' asked Clare, keenly.

'Can ye fuck, no. Sorry guys, I've just told ye. Naw. Rules.'

Sandy tried to reason with the mild-mannered door ogre.

'Aw, come on mate, none of us are drunk, none of us are on drugs, we just wanna dance, just let us in, pal, eh, please?' he pleaded.

The bouncer looked slightly annoyed but not genuinely pissed off, thankfully.

'Look, it's after curfew. You, my friend, are dressed like a throwback from an 80s acid-house party.' Sandy had to give him that one – because he was. The bouncer continued.

'The rest of ye do meet our dress code requirements, except you are covered in grass and mud stains, and the milky bar kid here [Kevin] looks like he's just been in a fight, look at all the blood on his mouth, add that to that the fact I can smell hash off you all so, regrettably, naw, *defense d'entrer*, no entry, no' the night, no' at this time, got it?'

And with that, the bouncer turned and strode back inside the club.

The friends stood there, deflated, frustrated. Just a few yards from the sweatbox dancefloor that they craved so much, yet so far from it, now, too.

The big, attractive female bouncer had been talking on her phone and smoking a cigarette while the debate with her colleague on the steps had taken place. When her male colleague retired back inside the venue, she stubbed out her fag on the wall and ended her phone call, then approached the six friends. At first glance she looked strong and intimidating, but her soft black hair, big blue eyes and the fact that closer sly visual examination by the guys hinted that under her big unflattering coat she was doubtless hiding the kind of body that makes men drool, made her far more approachable than her colleague.

'So, guys, you two are expecting? When are ye due? Ah'm Wendy, by the way.'

Kirsty and Clare were hesitant, looking at each other, before Kirsty answered, with an innocent smile.

'Eh, in about nine months, Wendy.'

'Oh right,' said Wendy. 'I see. So, what's he no' lettin' ye in for? You're regulars are ye no'?'

'He says we're too late and we're all covered in mud, I mean, can you believe that?' Said Sandy, smiling at Wendy, giving her *the look*, himself unsure if Wendy was genuinely giving him the glad-eye or if she was simply stunned at his 'retro' clothing from 1989.

The friends stood at the steps of that Bathgate nightclub, having been through so much together, desperate for some release, some music, some escape, some manumission.

Wendy lit up another cigarette – staff weren't allowed to smoke inside the club – then ran her keen eye over this motley crew of charming, passive, incredibly muddy, incredibly stoned young people. Her eyes met with Sandy's, then they disengaged, and she surveyed the friends once more, taking a long draw from her fag, then exhaling slowly, before asking:

'So, where did all this mud come fae?'

The friends all looked at each other, Stevie and Kev giggled a bit, Colin let out a long hiss – the type of hiss that some robbing bastard of a builder or a car mechanic might make while assessing the damage and thinking up a repair quote for you.

Sandy spoke next.

'Wendy, listen, these lovely people rescued me tonight. I was trapped in a tree up at Beecraigs Country Park for ten years, you see, some bastard had turned me into a wood fairy. But tonight, these guys rescued me, and to thank them, I threw a very bad person into a huge pile of cow shit. Before I was turned into a wood fairy, I'd been on the best weekend; Hacienda in Manchester on the Friday, then a big outdoor party in Glasgow on the Saturday, where I totally humiliated a bullying gangster. We never made it to the third destination, an outdoor rave in Edinburgh, though. I was hoping that, tonight, we could make up for that, a bit. Come on, Wendy, let us in, pleeease? Let us all celebrate the beauty of life.'

Everybody put on innocent smiling cherub faces and looked expectantly in hope at Wendy, the sexy bouncer. Wendy was quick to reply.

'Right then, you dae know that the Hacienda in Manchester had to close down in 1997, don't ye? It became a gangland murder hotspot. Shame, really, I was there a few times when I was younger, it was amazing, the best, in fact.'

Sandy lapped up that revelation enthusiastically and came straight back at her.

'Really? You were at The Hacienda? Wow, man, I was a student doon there, loved goin' there, what night did you go on? Who was the DJ? We quite liked going to *Nude* on Fridays, in fact, I even had tickets booked to see the Happy Mondays there on...'

'Ahem, Sandy, come on, man. She's no' lettin' us in, mate. Just leave it,' said Colin.

Sandy realised that he was rambling and that that probably wasn't helping them to gain entry to the club, he did, however, have the serious hots for the bouncer.

Wendy recapped it all.

'So, you're all here trying to get in after curfew, covered in mud, one of ye with a smashed-in mouth, and the reason you give the bouncer for all that is wood fairies, cow shit, the Hacienda and Beecraigs Country Park? Really?'

'Yes,' said Sandy aloud, as if crying Eureka.

Wendy the bouncer smiled and said, 'That's the biggest load of shite Ah've ever heard – that's pure dead brilliant. Well, in ye go then, fuck off, man – go on.' She nodded her head towards the door. They all practically bounced in the door, each stopping to give Wendy a big hug or a kiss on

BROKEN BISCUITS : THE WOOD FAIRY

the cheek. Wendy half laughed as they did. Sandy was the last to enter the club – Wendy whispered something in his ear as he gave her a hug and a peck on the cheek.

The six friends were elated. By then it was 1.30am but the club was still heaving, possibly 2000 punters were in, spread between the three rooms and the chillout area and foyer. The usual mix of young people were in, guys on speed playing fruit machines. Gaggles of young, beautiful women in short skirts and tight tops, small groups of sharply dressed young men wearing clobber equivalent in cost to two weeks wages for most people. Some people on drugs, others just drinking, many doing both, even a few doing neither. The beautiful people of central Scotland were out in force, up for a party. In the big room, the one where all the trance music was played, Nigel Benn, the former boxer, and George O'Dowd, better known as Boy George, were the headline acts. People love to go to clubs when a big famous DJ is on the bill, even more so when there are two on the bill, although, in the case of Bathgate's Room at the Top, the real stars were always, repeat *always*, the residents. DJ Tubbs in the cheese room, Martin Malone and Paul Mendez in the others – they were the real superstar DJs.

Sandy went to the bar and bought six ice-cold bottles of Highland Spring water for himself and his friends. He handed over a Bank of England £50 note which had the queen on one side and Sir Christopher Wren on the reverse. The barmaid looked at the note, puzzled, and swiped it with an anti-counterfeit marker and all was well. Sandy was relieved, as that was the only money that was left in his pockets, and that particular note had ceased to be legal tender in 1996. Win. He wished he'd bought Champagne, instead.

The friends were able to grab a wee table in the chillout and sit down while wee Kev, relishing being out in a club again, went in search of some pills – just four, though – none for Kirsty or Clare now. He soon returned with four speckled Mitsubishis, which he, Sandy, Stevie, and Colin gubbed. Their table was getting a few funny glances, probably because they were all covered in mud stains, but they didn't give a fuck. Besides, in a sweatbox you can't really comment on anyone else's appearance in a negative way, because by 4am, you'll all look like the living dead, anyway.

Sandy spoke to his new friends.

'Thanks, really. All of you. Listen, some of my ancestors were slaves in the Caribbean. Whenever a slave was freed by its master, the master furnished them with a document called a letter of manumission. This letter certified that the person was no longer a slave and was a free man, or a free woman. I love that word, *manumission*. In the future there'll probably be a famous nightclub called manumission and countless other club nights called that, and that's cool. But now, to me, for saving me, for freeing me, for giving me back my fuckin' life, man, you lot are my manumission. Thank you – you ended my slavery – you set me free.'

It was an emotionally charged moment. There was silence, then Colin piped up.

'That's awright, mate, thanks for helping us, too. We'd have been fucked without your help the night.' Kevin, Stevie, Clare, and Colin all nodded and smiled. A few handshakes were exchanged. Clare and then Kirsty each gave Sandy a big bear hug. Then Stevie spoke.

'One thing, Sandy, see since you escaped that tree, you're talking differently. You're more polite, well spoken, calm, how's that?'

'*Whit? Are you sayin' Ah was a fuckin' bad-tempered uncouth cunt when Ah wiz up the woods? So would you fuckin' be if you were stuck in a tree for fuckin' years – teapots – the lot ae ye.*' Sandy smiled broadly after blurting that out, in a much quieter mimic of how he had once sounded when they had all first met. That got everybody laughing. Then everyone heard two words spoken softly but loudly over the pumping bass coming from the main room– as did half of the people in the nightclub.

'DIVING FACES'

Sandy, Colin, Stevie, Kirsty, Clare, and wee Kev all got up and started dancing, whilst simultaneously moving from the chillout area through to the middle of the packed dancefloor in the main room. Lasers shone, smoke rose, strobe lights rippled and a thousand loved-up clubbers gave it laldy to Liquid Child's modern classic vocal trance anthem.

My thoughts pass away with the coming sea
All the faces around it was a wisdom for me
Follow my proclamation for a new experience of life
Don't be afraid, we now start to dive
For the liquid child, for a labyrinth of time
So open up your eyes and realize my sign
Come with me to the different places
And be a part of diving faces.

They rocked it out in the club until 4am, then went back to Kirsty's place, as per usual. All except Sandy, who went home with that female bouncer for some rip-roaring, biblical epic sex – after all – Sandy had ten years of spunk saved up.

And, with that, our six friends got their manumission, together, they were free – more free than they would ever be in their lives again. All was happy, all was well.

They were all some of life's broken biscuits, but they were now doing just fine in 1999.

Chapter Twenty-Six

CODA

On the Tuesday, reinstated disgruntled forest ranger, Ronnie Muir, was sent back up to Beecraigs by his bosses, whereupon, as ordered, he cut down a large, unstable beech tree, to make way for a new kiddies play area. He did this with some trepidation, still unsure whether or not he had imagined some of the weekend's events, and sure that, even if he hadn't imagined them, no cunt would believe him if he told them, anyway. The tree was taken away on a lorry. Soon after, Ronnie Muir and his wife moved up to Lochaber, where Ronnie had gotten a job with the Forestry Commission, and they were happy up there, too.

The morning after the beech tree was cut down and removed, an early-morning dog-walker in Beecraigs Country Park stumbled upon a gruesome sight. Local hated gangster and drug pusher, Gavin Kerr, was found lying dead near the picnic area. There was no blood on his body, near it, or anywhere else in the park for that matter. The body was also severed in two at the waist. There were no other injuries. No murder weapon. There was no explanation. SOCO officers and later pathologists were mystified. The police put it down to a gangland thing and never really pressed their investigation, glad to be rid of this scumbag once and for all. Their only suspect had been an associate of Kerr's, a William Carson Forbes, a man who claimed to have flown from Beecraigs to Mid Calder on the night in question, and who also claimed to have been attacked by fairies and talking trees up in the woods. Eyewitnesses who saw Carson in Mid Calder rolling about in cow shit on the night in question, the night that Kerr died, put Carson in the clear, though, so, the police closed the case.

Strange things can happen, up the woods, especially if you meet a wood fairy...

ABOUT THE AUTHOR

Ian is originally from Livingston, West Lothian. He had a nine-year career in warehousing before losing his legs in a fire, aged 24, in 2002. After that tragedy he became a writer, historian and actor. In 2023 he was diagnosed AuDHD.

www.ingramcontent.com/pod-product-compliance
Ingram Content Group UK Ltd.
Pitfield, Milton Keynes, MK11 3LW, UK
UKHW040712040825
7208UKWH00046B/460